USA Today Best Selling Author
Ashley Zakrzewski

Copyright © 2022 by Ashley Zakrzewski

All rights reserved.

No part of this book may be reproduced in any form or by any electronic or mechanical means, including information storage and retrieval systems, without written permission from the author, except for the use of brief quotations in a book review.

CONTENTS

1. Carleigh — 1
2. Bryson — 9
3. Carleigh — 17
4. Bryson — 23
5. Carleigh — 29
6. Bryson — 35
7. Carleigh — 39
8. Bryson — 53
9. Carleigh — 67
10. Carleigh — 83
11. Bryson — 93
12. Carleigh — 105
13. Carleigh — 115
14. Bryson — 131
15. Bryson — 139
16. Carleigh — 151
17. Carleigh — 163
18. Carleigh — 173
19. Bryson — 179
20. Carleigh — 191
21. Carleigh — 201
22. Bryson — 207
23. Carleigh — 213
24. Carleigh — 219

About the Author — 227

1
CARLEIGH

In the midst of April, Trinity up and leaves mid-degree on a free-spirited whim to go on a year-long backpacking trip in Southeast Asia, leaving me with a two-bedroom condo in Hell's Kitchen. It's nice, but not cheap enough for me to live in by myself, even with a little of my parents support. So, I put up on social media my need for a new roommate. Alarming place to do that, I know, but my profile is private so only my friends will see my plea. I refuse to ask my parents for a handout. It's been almost a year since my last request, and I'd like to keep it that way.

My father is a well-known pathologist and professor at Harvard. He and my mother have always pressed the virtues of hard work, earning my place, and paying my own way. They've helped, of course - it's a nicer apartment than a twenty-four-year-old should have - but it's only feasible if I have a roommate. My parents make it their mission to make sure my sister and I don't end up spoiled rich kids, despite our unavoidable privilege. As a logical person, it's better for me in every way that I acknowledge it and go my own way, as Stevie Nicks would say, but there are times when I'm on the subway home from my part-time serving job, only to have to write a paper into the wee hours once I get there, that I wish they were a little looser.

I pride myself on not having to run to my parents for money and work to provide for my place. It's not much, but it's mine. I've had a few years to spruce the place up a bit, and Trinity never appreciated my effort. An apartment shouldn't be a prison, and when I moved in, all it had was white walls, and that's the first thing I altered.

Colors remind us of enjoyment, and when I'm stuck at home, I need something that is soothing. The bedrooms are a soft blue, and the living room is a beige. Instead of painting it the same color as the bedrooms, I went with using furniture to accent the color scheme.

After a week with no offers, I panic. Rent is outstanding and I'm still three-hundred bucks short. I try to pick up a couple of extra shifts at work, but none are vacant. What am I going to do? There has to be someone out there needing a place to live.

When I first met Trinity, we got along efficiently. Same as now, I couldn't be picky about who moved in, and so I went with the first woman that applied. We were attending the same college, and that would keep her busy with her thesis instead of causing drama. Even with her, it was a transition.

I'm a spotless and organized person and like things a certain way, and she never criticized, happy to follow my lead. I have a right to be agitated about Trinity deserting me, since we agreed to live together throughout all of grad school, not three-quarters of it. It's the sort of thing I like the idea of doing if I were a different person, someone without twenty-four years of deep-seated anxiety, perfectionism, and high expectations drilled into me. The world needs people like Trinity to follow their hearts just as much as it needs people like me to rigidly follow their five-year plans.

Some people make fun of me because I like to make lists. There is something so gratifying with being able to mark something off when it's complete. My compulsion started when I was nine- years-old, and I got my first planner. In the back, there were three to five lined pages for whatever, and I used them to write my goals. Silly, right? A nine-year-old with goals? Trinity used to get mad about how organized I am, but it's because she couldn't keep to a schedule to save her life. Grad school is savage and the only way anyone graduates is by staying in their lane and keeping to a very strict schedule. My parents have pushed me to become someone who changes the world for the better, gives back to the community, and makes them proud. No way I'm going to throw all my hard work away just to go backpacking. *Absurd.*

I couldn't even tell you the last time I went on a vacation. Possibly, before I graduated from high school. Since then, I have put all my focus on school and getting my Master's degree. I'm the girl everyone makes fun of for having a stick up their butt. School has always been my priority and, with me being on the home stretch, there is no time for distractions. Just a couple more months and I will have achieved one of my parents' goals for me.

Still, the new roommate thing is troublesome. I don't want to teach somebody new my methods. The rent on the apartment is reasonable for the location, a thousand bucks a month, and it's in the middle of the city. This makes getting places much easier. Why hasn't anyone expressed interest?

My phone buzzes on the coffee table behind my laptop, and I check it.

Evan: Let's meet on campus for coffee

He's a college friend, and it'll be nice to get a minor break from my thesis. We haven't hung out in a couple months because the last semester of grad school is killer, and it's important to keep our eyes on the prize.

Me: On my way

I close my laptop, then dash to the bedroom to put on some jean shorts and a t-shirt. My mother would have a conniption fit if I went anywhere public in sweats. Sometimes, I wish I didn't have rich parents, because then I could wear whatever I want, and not have to be in the spotlight.

I stride out of the front doors of the building, and the hustle and bustle of New York is vast. Cars are honking and people are sauntering up and down the sidewalk. The noise is overwhelming if you aren't used to it. I head out toward the campus, which is only a couple of blocks.

Students are studying on the grass, books splayed out on a blanket, some are throwing a football around, or flirting with their boyfriends. See, I don't have time for all this nonsense. Graduating is the most important thing to me, and how they find the time to be so social is beyond me.

I stroll inside the quad and see Evan relaxing at a table. The coffee shop is almost full when I arrive. There is someone at every table, but to their merit, it is the best coffee on campus. Caffeine is the only legal thing that keeps students awake to study their hearts out. Many of them have headphones on, which is normal. It's not possible to sit in here and get any work done, because it's so loud.

"Hey, you!" Evan says, standing up to give me a hug. "It's been way too long."

I nod and take a seat across from him.

My parents love Evan because he comes from a semi-wealthy family himself. I have tried to explain that we are just friends, but they have a one-track mind. It's important to them that I marry the right person, and to them it's money. I understand they don't want me or my future children to struggle, but marriage is about love. I'm not going to just marry someone because they have money.

"Sucks about Trinity. Or does it? Were you guys friends? I couldn't ever tell."

Things are complicated. I've never wanted to live with friends, because most people get annoyed with how particular I am about certain things. No dishes left in the sink. No dirty clothes left on the bathroom floor. I like to keep a spotless environment.

"Friends or not. She abandoned me without covering her rent for this month. So now, I have to shell out almost a grand somehow."

I take a sip of my Caramel Macchiato and roll my eyes, miffed at Trinity still for putting me in this predicament. She could have waited until the end of the month, but maybe she didn't want to pay her half of the rent. Trip money, I suppose.

"Just bite the bullet and ask your parents. It's not like they are going to say no. How would that look if you get evicted?" He tilts his head and shrugs his shoulders.

The difference between Evan and myself is that he isn't afraid to ask his parents for money. In fact, he gets a weekly allowance deposited into his account. Mine, however, have clarified that I don't get access to my trust fund until after I finish grad school and get married.

"Well, my friend Bryson is interested. Doesn't mind a roommate. You remember him?"

I put my hand up, and almost choke on my coffee. "Bryson? You've got to be kidding me. I'm not living with a man. My parents would freak out."

"Jesus, grow up, Carleigh. He's not going to try to screw you. Bryson just needs a place to live that's closer to his job, and your apartment is like ten minutes from it. He has to get on a ferry every day right now."

Living with a man never even crossed my mind, but I'm desperate right now. I'm almost three-hundred bucks short on the rent this month, and I refuse to ask my parents for money.

"Can he pay the first month and last month's rent?"

Evan nods.

"Fine. Tell him we will do a trial run. Two months."

I don't want to live with a man, but right now I don't have people fighting to be my roommate. The rent has to be paid this week and I'm short. Bryson is the only way it gets paid.

He isn't a total stranger to me. I met Bryson before through Evan. He dresses like a fisherman and works construction, so it's clear he will be good at all the practical things I'm not. Bryson is charming easily, and he even seemed to like me well enough - not always a guarantee with my prickly personality.

"He is asking if he can move in tomorrow?"

Wow, he moves fast, doesn't he? I must not be the only one that's desperate. "Yeah, if he wants to bring the two thousand with him tomorrow. I can be at the apartment by one."

Evan vigorously types back and then grins. "Great. He said see you at one. Talk to you soon."

He saunters off to his next class, and I go back to my apartment to finish working on my thesis. It is the reason for my never-ending headaches, and I'll be ecstatic once it's complete.

My mind isn't focusing on writing, but on my soon to be roommate. What if we clash from the start? After he pays me, I won't be able to kick him out. Desperate times call for desperate measures, and no matter what happens, I'll just have to suck it up for at least two months.

Bryson isn't that dreadful, right?

2
BRYSON

The commute from New Jersey to Manhattan is despicable. Between the early morning ferries and living in-between roommates out of my mom's basement, it is really getting to me. I've been trying to find a place in Manhattan for a couple of months with no luck. Everything is like a grand a month, and I'm not willing to spend that much on an apartment. My search keeps coming up dry.

My mother rents her house out for tourists and makes a killing. She is lucky enough to be able to stay at my aunt's house while it's rented, but there isn't enough room for me. My friends are getting sick of me crashing on their couches, and the search for an apartment has come up empty.

The aroma coming from the kitchen is divine, and only cements how much I'll miss her home-cooked meals.

"Freshly cooked bacon is how I want to start every day," I say, kissing her on the cheek.

My mother and I are tight and I wouldn't have it any

other way. She likes to meddle in my love life, but it's to be expected. It's not like I'm in my late thirties or something. Why should I be in a rush to settle down and have a family?

"Any luck on apartments, son?" she asks, fixing some bacon on a plate with scrambled eggs and setting it down on the kitchen table in front of me.

I take my fork and take a bite of eggs first. "The prices for apartments over there are insane. I might be here another week."

She hasn't explicitly come out and told me I need to leave, but the gentle nudges are enough.

"If you find yourself a nice girl, then maybe you could buy a house. Less money wasted."

As much as I would love to own a home, it's out of the cards for me right now. I just don't make enough, but when the foreman manager position comes open, I hope they recommend me. I've been sure to work as much as possible, and keep my head down. If I get the promotion, the bump in salary will help me afford an apartment by myself, but there's no telling when they will open the position.

My fork clinks around the plate as I scoop up eggs and force them into my mouth. I wish I could sleep in every once in a while, but it's about an hour commute to work, and they don't take kindly to tardiness.

"A happy plate. Have a good day, son."

I take my bag and put it around my shoulders. "I'll see you later, ma."

The trek to the boarding station for the ferry is about a mile, and there is really no point in driving and parking. The cost is an unnecessary expense, and it's excellent exercise. Kids are playing in the street, and they always say good morning to me. A couple of them I went to school with their parents, and it surprises me that they have little ones already.

By the time I get to the loading dock, my shirt is wet from the cardio. It's an easy way to keep in shape these days.

"One for Manhattan, please."

The agent hands me my ticket, and I board the ferry. The view is beautiful, but after seeing it every day you lose appreciation for it. Tourists only dream of visiting the big city skyscrapers and bustling city. There are things that even patrons of the city might not be aware of, but it's because they want to be oblivious. The rich people are only driving up the living expenses, and contractors are making a killing. Take Brooklyn, for example. My boss signed a million dollar contract for the building, and they will turn it into fifteen floors of condos, then they will probably sell for about half a million each. Sometimes, people come in and want to help better a neighborhood, but that means they usually buy out the rest of it to withhold the aesthetic.

Lawyers are approaching patrons of the neighborhood that have been there for decades, and offering to buy them out so they can bulldoze their property and make room for new properties. It is a lower income neighborhood, and most can't afford to turn down a deal that is three times what the house is worth. I in no way blame them, but it's just a dirty deal. So many memories in these houses, yet they are being torn down to build new condos and skyscrapers.

My eyes set on the city skyline, and see all the new developments going up, and even though I get paid pretty good, sometimes the guilt is too much. They want to continuously put up new properties, and I understand that's how they make their money, but sometimes I wish we could just leave some neighborhoods alone. Offering two-hundred thousand dollars for a house that's not even worth a hundred is good business, but what are they going to do with that money?

The ferry comes to my stop, and I depart, wondering what the day might bring. Will they finally announce the new position? Our current Foreman Manager has taken a new job opportunity with a different company, and he is only with us for another couple of weeks. I would think they would want to give the new manager time to get settled in before he leaves, but who knows?

It's about a ten-minute walk to the worksite, and my shirt is soaked at this point. When I approach, there are only a handful of guys standing around and the start time is in fifteen-minutes. Where is everybody?

"Hey, Bryson, what's the deal? Where is everyone at?"

I shrug my shoulders. It's funny that they would think I would have a clue. I'm not in the know.

About that time, Blake steps out of his trailer, and asks us to gather around. Does this mean they have finally made a decision? I cross my fingers, and my anxiety kicks up.

"As you know, I've accepted a job at another company and they would like to promote from within. You have all done some amazing work for the company, but they have made their decision. Bryson, they have chosen you to be the new Foreman Manager. Come see me so we can get the paperwork submitted," Blake says, going back inside.

I try not to jump up and down with joy in front of everyone, because there are some guys that have been here longer than me. No need to rub it in their faces. Two guys pat me on the back and congratulate me on the way to Blake's office.

My hand reaches for the door, and it opens revealing Blake with a smile. "Come on in. We have a lot to talk about."

I step inside and browse around. He has family pictures up on the walls and an open floor plan that is mostly used for his office.

"Have a seat. Let me grab the paperwork and we will go over it."

I sit in front of his desk, and take in the pictures. We don't talk about our personal lives much on the job, but I am surprised to learn that he has kids. He has never mentioned them.

"Beautiful family, sir. Are they excited about the move?"

He shakes his hand. "My wife isn't happy about the transition, but once the first paycheck hits, she'll understand why I took it. We are expecting our third child and we just couldn't make it off what I make a week. I can't expect her to go back to work, because then we would have to figure out daycare and that shit is pricey."

"Okay, you just need to sign where it's highlighted. It has all the benefits and salary information on it." He leans back in his chair and stretches out.

The front displays my new health insurance plan, 401K, and last, but not least, the pay. I almost take a second glance because I'm a little taken back. Eighty-nine thousand.

"Everything satisfactory?" he asks, watching the pen hover over the place to sign my name.

"Yeah, of course."

I sign the line and push the paper back across the desk. This is going to change my life, and I might finally be able to get my own apartment in a couple months, but what do I do until then?

"You can go back out there with the crew. We'll talk more later."

I nod, and retreat to the worksite, joining the other men in bulldozing the newest house to sign the buy-out agreement. There are ten houses on this block and they are trying to get all of them to reconsider their offer. It will only work if they have the whole block to build new properties, but there are a couple people who refuse to move. Good for them.

My phone buzzes in my pocket, and I remove my work gloves and take it out.

Evan: One of my friends is looking for a roommate. Hell's Kitchen. $500 a month.

Is this finally going to be the day I get to move back out of my mother's house? How am I ever going to find a woman if I'm living with my mother? My job provides me with security so I don't have the fear of losing my job. Especially now.

Me: What's the catch?

The three dots appear, and I anxiously await his answer. The bubble pop noise plays.

Evan: It's Carleigh. I don't know if you remember her, but her roommate up and abandoned her.

Hell's Kitchen would be perfect since my jobs are primarily in Manhattan or Brooklyn, and while getting to Manhattan is one thing, Brooklyn days have been tougher. And only getting worse.

Carleigh Murphy. She didn't care for me when I met her once or twice. I get it. I'm loud and a little hyperactive, probably give off a stupid-masculine vibe, and not everyone's cup of tea. Especially, not someone like Carleigh, who seems very studious. Not at all the kind of person who's interested in dealing with a lot of energy being thrown her way. I remember her being polite but quiet, a closed book with a very obvious perfectionist cover, and didn't get any of my movie references. *What a damn shame.*

We are clearly from different worlds.

But hey, I've got an open mind. Plus - not to be braggy, but it is kind of true – I get along with most people just fine. I'm easy going and don't get stressed out easily, not to mention pretty confident as long as Carleigh stands me. I can deal with any idiosyncrasies she might have.

Me: First and last month's rent? Can I move in tomorrow?

It's my day off, and I don't want to wait another week. Plus, if we give her more time for someone else to be interested, she will probably go with them.

Evan: She will be at the apartment at one tomorrow. Bring the cash with you.

I slip my gloves back on, and slide the phone back into my pocket and get back to work. This is the best news I have received in a while. Honestly, I'm surprised Carleigh considered me for a roommate, but maybe I didn't repulse her as badly as I remember.

As long as we stay in our separate rooms, what could go wrong?

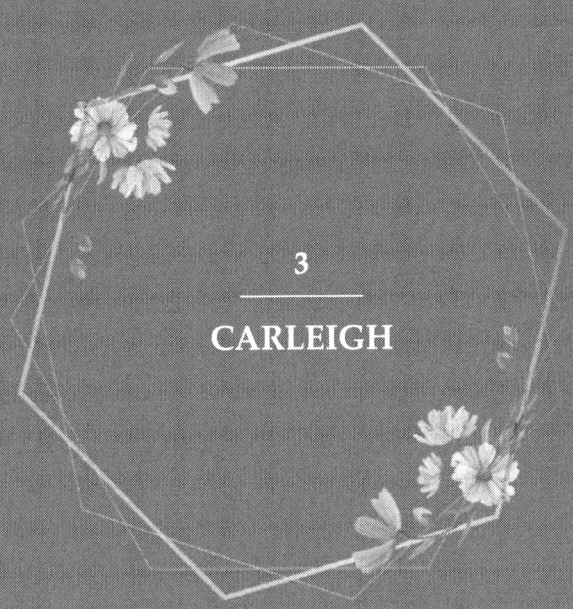

3
CARLEIGH

My anxiety is already through the roof from a man moving into my apartment today, but it's Bryson. What if he is a slob? My OCD about cleanliness is non-negotiable and he will have to abide by my rules. I'm not changing them.

Bryson strikes me as the type to be bull-headed, and that's what scares me the most. I don't want to butt heads with him every day. Trinity and I weren't perfect, but we rarely had issues.

My class ends promptly around twelve-thirty and I go straight to the coffee shop to grab a latte and a caramel macchiato. The only thing I remember from our first encounter is his coffee order. A vanilla latte with two shots of espresso. I figure it will be a friendly gesture to prepare him to move in with a warm cup of coffee. Or will he read more into it?

I second guess myself, walking the five blocks to the apartment. Should I ditch the coffee altogether? *Stop being overdramatic.* My feet begin up the stairs to the third floor, and when I open the door to exit to the foyer, Bryson is standing in front of the apartment.

"Hey, you're early." I say, picking up speed. He is standing with a backpack and two duffel bags in his hands.

"Yeah, it's a habit. Never know when the ferry might leave late, so I always give myself extra time to be safe."

I sit the two coffees on the floor, and take the key out of my pocket. "There you go."

After retrieving the cups, I use my foot to close the door and then set them down on the kitchen island. "I got you a latte, if you want it. Might not be as hot now, but still warm."

He nods, and looks around the place. Everything is in its respective place. Will he say anything about how tidy the apartment is? My parents always comment on it when they show up unannounced.

"So, where's my room?" He glances around the living room, not really showing any facial expressions.

"Right through here."

I open the door and let him set his bags down. His arms must be throbbing. How long was he standing out there like that?

He unpacks his bags, throwing things into the six drawer cherry oak dresser that Trinity left behind. Why he is wanting to move in so quickly? It's not like I'm in a position to question it, since the landlord should be over any minute to collect the rent.

"Did you bring the money?"

I didn't want to ask so suddenly, but might as well get it out of the way. He will want to settle in and get things put away, and I doubt he wants to be interrupted when he shows up.

He pulls out a wad of cash from his backpack and hands it to me.

"Do you know how dangerous it is to walk around with that kind of money? You could've been robbed for gosh sakes."

He shrugs his shoulders and then looks at his arms. "Doubt anyone would try anything with me."

So, he has an ego. Noted. I hope he isn't one of those guys that bring home a different girl every night, because I don't want to listen to him screwing chicks.

"So, maybe we should talk about the rules. Yeah?"

He doesn't stop unpacking things, and so I just start laying them out. "If you use a dish, wash it when you are done. No dirty dishes left in the sink. Same with clothes. If you take a shower, throw the clothes into the hamper in your room or into the washer."

He stops what he's doing, and turns to face me. "We know nothing about each other, but I'm not a slob. You don't have to worry about me. I'll barely be here. No need to worry about me, Carleigh."

The way he says my name almost interprets him as being condescending, but maybe I'm reading too much into it.

"I am gone often, too. Trinity was good about keeping things organized in my absence and I expect you to do the same. If so, we will get along great."

He doesn't respond, and that leads to me leaving his room and going to the kitchen. I have some time to make blueberry turnovers, and baking always helps me to destress. There is nothing like putting in the work to taste a masterpiece at the end. Trinity always raved me up about how good my baking skills were, and there for a while, I wanted to pursue culinary school, but my parents would never go for it.

I pull out my pastry dough and the fresh blueberries from the fridge. I preheat the oven and line two baking sheets with parchment paper.

"Let me know if you need anything," I yell loud enough so he can hear me, as I stretch to reach the sauce pan necessary to make the blueberry sauce.

I take about five minutes to gather the other ingredients and then throw things into a small mixing bowl. The trick is you have to let the mixture heat over medium until it gets not only nice and bubbly, but thick enough. This usually takes about three to four minutes, and then I let it cool down while I prepare the dough.

The knife settles in my hand and I cut up the pastry dough into squares, and add two tablespoons of the filling into the middle of the squares. You don't want to add too much or eating them will be messy.

"What are you making in here?" he asks, stepping into the kitchen.

"Blueberry turnovers."

He nods. "Where are the cups?"

I point to the cabinet next to the fridge and he gets a glass of water and goes back to his room.

Bryson doesn't seem as talkative as he normally is, or from what I remember during our encounters. The first time I met him with Evan, he talked about Marvel movies for almost an hour.

A whisk is used to mix water and eggs in a small bowl and I use a fork to close them before putting the mixtures on the top of them. Something I didn't know the first time I attempted to make these is you have to put some holes in the turnover for the steam to escape while they are cooking, or it doesn't turn out correctly.

The oven beeps, startling me. It's up to the right temperature and I slide them in. I utilize the cooking time to go over my thesis again. Over the last two days, I have been able to go through about ten pages. At this rate, I'll finish the revision stage in two weeks.

It's so quiet in the apartment, I almost forget that Bryson is here until he scares the crap out of me. "What are you doing?"

He throws his hands up in the air. "Sorry. Just looking at what you are working on. I tried to ask, but you didn't even hear me."

He hasn't even been here an entire day yet, and he's already snooping on my stuff. "It's my thesis, and it's not for anyone else to read right now."

The oven beeps, and I rush over to take the pastries out of the oven and use the brush to run the glaze over the top.

It is here, though, that I must register a complaint: he's not really a dessert person.

"Carleigh, I don't know what to tell you."

Seriously? I just stare at him blankly after he'd declined one of my amazing blueberry turnovers.

"Everyone is a dessert person, Bryson."

"No. Not me." He'd cheerfully prodded a nearby jar of what will be pickles, which sit atop a small shelf he'd brought with him and named the fermentation station.

Letting things rot in jars, apparently, is one of his

hobbies. Although, it's kind of unsightly, I will allow this - only because I love pickles.

This is fine in and of itself: I force nobody to like sugary treats, and I'm not in the business of force-feeding people my food. Unfortunately, we have a very Manhattan-sized freezer, and I am quickly running out of room to house leftover baking. Trinity used to take a lot, her sweet tooth was legendary, so without my main recipient, the pile in the freezer is growing. I can eat some of it myself obviously, but I've been pushing myself to start eating a little better since I signed up for a marathon in August.

There is a knock at the door, and he walks to answer it, but I walk in front of him and shake my head. "I'll answer it."

His neck cocks back as he rolls his eyes and then walks away. "You are a feisty one, aren't you?"

Just as I predicted, Bryson and I are going to squabble. It's only a matter of time, but right now I'm focused on not getting evicted. Another knock and I open the door.

"You said you had the rent ready?" the older man says, reaching out his hand.

"Sure did. Here you go!"

He counts it, and writes out a receipt. "I'll see you next month."

I shut the door and lean against it, finally able to catch my breath. Bryson might be a pain, but without him, I wouldn't have a place to live after tomorrow. He doesn't know this, and I'll never tell him, but I take a minute to be thankful for that.

4

BRYSON

The first week of settling into the apartment flies by, and Carleigh and I rarely even see each other. When we do, it's amicable, but she's a lot less uptight than I expect her to be. I feel bad for making that assumption, even if I never voiced it to anyone else. But hey, if it's the thought that counts, then a bad thought has to count, too, right?

She makes me the most popular guy at work every day, when I turn up with another batch of whatever she's been experimenting with baking lately - even if I don't love that the Bryson-brings-baking praise sometimes comes with a kind of passive toxic masculinity, from a couple of rotten-apple coworkers I've spent my life proving I'm not like. Just because I like hunting, fishing, and fixing stuff doesn't mean I'm a sexist asshole. Or, that I'm cool putting up with it from other people who give outdoorsy guys like me a bad name.

On the day before my birthday, I show up to work with a container of Carleigh's flaky, buttery homemade croissants and one of the younger guys tells me to get Carleigh to make them some doughnuts. This annoys me right off the bat: clearly, the baking is a free gift. Besides, Carleigh's croissants are incredible. I purposely left half a dozen behind at home that morning for my own consumption.

"She'll make whatever she wants, and if you're lucky, I get to bring some of it," I inform him.

"Oh, come on, Bryson. Lay some good pipe and right after, ask her for doughnuts. I bet she'd make some damn good ones."

I give him my best *what the hell* face. "She's just my roommate, you moron, there isn't - "

"Oh, y'all aren't doing the deed? Can I have her number, then?"

"What? No! You don't even know anything about her."

The younger guy shrugs. "Anyone who has the patience to make something like this probably has a lot she wants to prove in bed, you know?"

"No, I don't know," I say sharply. "Now move off over there, shift's starting."

While I pride myself on maintaining a positive attitude, this puts a bit of a damper on my mood for the rest of the day. I don't mind construction work most of the time, as unfulfilling as it is, but it's days like this and guys like whatever-his-name-is that really make me want to get the hell out of the industry.

Carleigh's not there when I get home from work, which really isn't much of a surprise. She's in school and also works a part-time job at a bar somewhere, and I've been spending a lot of evenings out with friends in the city now that I'm not married to ferry schedules. The usual routine commences -

a shower and a shave to wash off the dirt and sweat of my day job - and I am in the middle of checking on a couple of fermentation projects when the apartment door opens and Carleigh comes in.

She's just been on a run, I gather. She's sweaty and half-breathless, wearing running shoes, a white tank top that somehow only makes her more pale, and a pair of floral gray leggings I recognize from a clothes hamper. She's been training for a marathon; I've seen a decent amount of athletic wear in our tiny laundry space, after all, but I'm not home a lot and haven't had a lot of opportunity to see that athletic wear on her.

And look, I'm more evolved than the average Jersey ding-bat, okay? I've read *Little Women*, and not for a school project. But right now, in the kitchen, *damn*.

Carleigh is beautiful. That much was obvious as soon as I met her: big, dark eyes, a strangely alluring streak of gray at the front of her hair, and a lot of pale, unblemished skin I can just tell is soft. And while she dresses pretty casually, it's also clear there are some nice curves under her jeans and loose-fitting shirts.

I'm not staring at her ass, okay? She just so happens to be tying her shoes while I'm standing in the kitchen, holding a jar of sauerkraut, and if I observe the shape of her calves, thighs, and hips... Okay maybe I'm staring.

Damn it. I'm just another idiot like ol' what's-his-face from this morning, thinking dirty things about Carleigh just because she's wearing pants that make it clear just how great her ass is. *Be better than this, Bryson.*

She's still wearing ear buds in her ears and obviously hasn't noticed me standing here. So, I clear my throat and wave in her direction with my clean hand, counting on the fact of my general largeness to ensure she sees me.

When she does, she startles a little and lets out a soft, "oh!" noise. Carleigh reaches up, takes the earbuds out of her ears, and gives me a sheepish smile. "Hi, didn't see you there."

"Sorry, didn't want to scare you."

"Oh, it's my fault, I should've turned off my music." She sets her phone and earbuds down on the counter, then pours herself a glass of water. She guzzles it without stopping, then pours another and downs that as well, which makes me chuckle.

"Ever thought about bringing water with you while you run?"

Carleigh walks past me and sinks into a chair next to my Fermentation Station. "I've tried all the different bottles, blenders, and everything. I just don't like it. It's bad enough to bring my phone and keys with me, but that's kind of necessary."

"Fair enough." I grab a jar of what will be garlic and ginger paste. "How was the run?"

"It was good!" Carleigh pulls her phone toward her and taps a few times on the screen. "I'm on pace for where I want to be, I think. Hmm, yeah," she continues, peering at what I assume is a tracking app. "Not bad considering mid-afternoon isn't my best time of day. How was work?"

I paste on a smile. "Another day in paradise!"

"How'd the croissants go over?" she asks, her face scrunching up curiously. "Any feedback?"

I point to the empty container in the sink. "Gone by eight thirty. That's all the feedback you need."

"You kept a couple here."

I grin. "Yeah, I love croissants. You can make them savory. They aren't desserts like your cakes."

"Interesting, I'll remember that," she comments, smiling. "Likes croissants. I make a good cheese croissant. I'll have to whip some up for you to try next weekend or something." She pulls her phone off the table. "I should go shower, probably. God, I still can't believe you don't like cake. What do you do on your birthday?"

"Sometimes I have pie, I do like pie. Sometimes, we just don't have dessert." I hesitate before adding, "Tomorrow's actually my birthday, so I just won't have it. You don't have to have cake to make it a good birthday."

Her eyebrows shoot up. "Tomorrow's your birthday? Bryson! Why didn't you say something?"

I shrug and hold my hands up. "I don't know! It isn't a big deal."

"So, are you going home to Jersey?"

I nod. "Yeah, but not 'til the weekend. Then my sister can be there with her kids and all that."

Carleigh chews on her bottom lip. "So, big plans for your birthday in the city, then?"

"Not really. A couple of friends might meet me for a drink later, like eight-ish. But nothing wild." I snap my fingers. "You should come out. Meet some of the gang. I think it's Quinn and maybe Bishop-"

"That sounds fun, but I actually work tomorrow," Carleigh says apologetically. "And today, actually, I should get going." She gets up from the table and takes a few steps toward the hallway. "Thirsty Thursdays, we have good deals on pints of the house lager. But, if you have nothing major going on for supper, try to save some room - I'll leave you a birthday pastry before I go to work. I promise you'll like it."

I grin again, curious what it'd be. Still, I politely decline. "Oh, you don't have to do that."

"I want to. It's your birthday!" Carleigh sets her water glass in the sink. "Anyway, now I definitely need to hop in the shower before I go to work. Hope you left lots of hot water!"

"No promises!" I call after her retreating figure, waiting for the bathroom door to shut, then look back at my fermenting garlic, grinning.

The next day, I go out for a post-work birthday drink with a couple of the guys from my crew. By the time I get home, Carleigh is already gone, but there's a note on the table that says look in the fridge.

In the fridge is a small pot pie, less than six inches across, made with Carleigh's perfect flaky pastry. It's wrapped neatly in plastic with another note on top. *Guinness and beef,* the note reads. *Reheat in the oven at 350 for twenty minutes.*

It's the best pie I've ever had.

5

CARLEIGH

There's a bit of an adjustment period. Bryson turns out to be a morning person, which wouldn't be bad, but he also turns out to be the kind of person who sings in the shower - and in the kitchen, the living room, and when he's getting dressed for work. Trinity was an early morning cyclist, so I invested in various sets of disposable earplugs, but Bryson's voice still permeates through. Sometimes, I find myself wanting to strangle him, but I resist. I'll have to buy a more reliable set, at least for nights when I don't have a morning class the next day.

His voice is also not the only thing that's loud. Everything about my new roommate is loud. His feet fall heavily on our vinyl flooring. He has a tendency to kind of lumber around, occasionally knocking into things. His laugh is boisterous, raised, the kind that I usually only hear from people in a large group, when other people's personalities turn up to eleven. Bryson only has one level.

Generally, though, it goes okay. Bryson's friendly, surprisingly organized, and has a pretty happening social life, so not home that much.

I work four evenings a week as a server at a low-key, hole-in-the-wall pub in the Financial District, and on those nights when I'm not getting home until after midnight, I usually have work to do on my grad school thesis – a thorough analysis of the role of food and cooking scenes in mid-century American Literature – or a baking project that I want to tackle.

After the first week of Bryson living with me, he solves my freezer problem.

It starts with a gentle knock on my bedroom door and a hesitant, "um, Carleigh?"

I look up from my annotated copy of *Cannery Row*, which I'm rereading in my favorite reading spot - the side of my bed that's pushed up against the window, reading pillow behind my back, cross-legged. "Yeah?"

Bryson nudges the door open. "I was - oh hey, turntable! Cool!" He steps into the space easily, taking only one long stride to reach my dresser, where my father's old record player sits. "What do you have on the go? Let me see - whoa Carleigh, Nebraska! Didn't peg you for being a fan of the Boss!"

It's about nine, on one of the rare evenings so far where we are both home, but I didn't plan on being social tonight because it's an aggressive redo-this-section schedule. But he lives here now and I've never really been social, which isn't really conducive to a positive cohabitation relationship. Even if we obviously have little in common and will never be best friends.

Still, we both like Springsteen, so that's something. I nod

and smile. "I've got a lot of his albums. Most are my dad's originally, the others I went hunting for in used record stores. You're a fan, I presume?"

"Of course, he's a Jersey boy!" Bryson gestures to the record player. "Can we turn it on? I haven't heard this bad boy in a good long while!"

The combination of his enthusiasm and somewhat odd manner of speaking makes me smile. "Sure, Bryson. Do you know how, or did you want me to?"

He waves me off. "Do I know how to use a record player, she asks. I'm not an animal! Don't you worry your pretty little head." He takes a minute, but soon enough the opening harmonica rings throughout the bedroom, and he turns to me with a wide grin.

"You look a little happy for how bleak this song is," I observe.

Bryson shrugs good-naturedly. "I'm just excited! I knew you had some surprises up your sleeve, Murphy. Not all Ivy League after all." He sits down on the floor, crosses his ankles, and hangs his wrists over his knees as he leans back, listening to the song. Five seconds after the lyrics begin, Bryson suddenly sits up and peers at me. "Nothing wrong with Ivy League, of course! Obviously. Just you know. Bruce is the working man's man, so I figured - not that you're not a working man, or lady, but -"

"It's okay," I cut in, smiling. I get it; I'm a fairly easy stereotype. Harvard undergrad, then Columbia, summer house in Cape Cod. "Whatever you assumed about me, it's probably mostly right."

Bryson shakes his head vigorously and holds his hands up, palms facing toward me. "I didn't assume anything!

Morocco said you were cool, that's the only assumption I made. I promise." He tilts his head and averts his eyes to my shelf, where my stack of records sit. "I did kind of figure you might be into opera or something, though."

"Opera!" I laugh. "I'm stuffy and uncool, but not that bad."

Bryson furrows his brow. "You aren't either of those things. I don't know you that well yet, but I know that much already. Being a hard worker doesn't make you either of those things."

I bite my lip. "Oh, well - thanks." I clear my throat, the weight of *Cannery Row* on my lap reminding me of tonight's to-do list. "Anyway, um, did you need something?"

"Oh, right!" Bryson claps his hands on his knees and springs to his feet. "I was wondering what the deal was with the freezer. It's kind of full."

"Oh." I make a face. "I'm taking more than my half. I'm kind of a stress baker, but I'm also sort of training for a marathon and can't eat it all myself, and you said you didn't really like dessert, so - I'm sorry, I promise I'll try harder to find it all a home."

"Oh, is that all you need? Just some people to eat it all?" Bryson snaps his fingers and points at me with one of them. "I got just the thing. I guarantee you if I bring it to the job site tomorrow, it'll all be gone by lunchtime."

That could work. I smile at him. "That actually sounds perfect. I'll package it up tonight, so it's easy to take with you tomorrow morning."

"Cool!" Bryson swings a foot backward, almost kicking over a pile of books. "Then there'll be room for pizza rolls!"

I wrinkle my nose. "Oh, Bryson, no. Don't buy those. I'll make you some homemade ones."

His eyes light up. "Homemade pizza rolls? You make those?"

"I haven't before, but it'll be a fun challenge." I'm always up for making new things, and love to take requests.

Bryson grins. "You make me pizza rolls, babe, I'll nominate you for roommate of the year."

I pick up my book again. "It's a deal," I say, smiling at the pages.

6

BRYSON

Things go well with my new living arrangement. She is down to earth. Her love of music is refreshing, because most people our age are into that rap crap, or Taylor Swift. The oldies are better for the soul, and even Carleigh knows it.

We rarely run into each other, our schedules don't coincide that often, but she left me a note that she made homemade pizza rolls in the freezer. It's wonderful she bakes, but it's never been my thing.

My phone buzzes against the kitchen island, and it's my mother.

"Hey, ma. I'm fixing to head that way." I hold the phone with my shoulder while I graze on a blackberry turnover.

"I'll have dinner ready. See you in a bit."

I am not a sweets person, and it doesn't stop her from trying to get me to taste her creations. So sometimes I give in when she isn't around, just in case I despise it. It turns out to be pretty good, so I grab another for the trip over and head out the door.

My mother says she has something she needs to talk to me about and normally I would be worried, but not today. Maybe she has finally decided to move closer to my aunt. She hates when I mention her age, but it's the truth. She's not getting any younger, and neither is her sister. They are both retired and might as well go enjoy their time. Why is she always at home when the world is her oyster?

The couple of blocks walk over to the boarding station for the ferry winds me, and honestly, it's just because since taking my new position, I don't get to be as hands on as I normally would. I need to get cardio again soon.

When I get to my mother's, my shirt is soaked but it is nice. Sweat means I'm burning calories.

"Hey, ma," I say, walking in the door, and finding her in the kitchen. She has always loved cooking and well, I like to eat.

"I made spaghetti for ya. Take a seat."

Even as an adult, she likes to sometimes treat me as if I'm a child, and meals are the worst. She refuses to let me make my own plate, instead she serves me like a waitress. "Ma, come on. I can do that."

"Not in my house. Eat up."

She sits down next to me, and starts shoveling food in her mouth. Her eyes keep glancing over to me almost like I'm not eating fast enough.

"So, what is the big news? You didn't ask me over just to have dinner. Spill."

She drops her fork, and finishes chewing before she starts talking to me about wanting to buy another house and rent it out. It's a wonderful idea, because she could always use extra money to travel to all the places on her bucket list.

"Where have you been looking? There is a neighborhood that is almost done in Manhattan. It's not the fancy condos, but you could probably rent them out for three or four hundred a night easily."

Buying property right now is smart. The construction over there is booming and once they finish doing the entire neighborhood, the market value for the structures will go up. Plus, she will be able to rent them out nightly and make a killing. It's a tourist area, and most times hotels are just too expensive for them. A condo is a cheaper option but makes it more like a home, too. You still have your own kitchen and living room without having to shell out money to have a suite at a hotel.

"I was wondering if you would point me in the right direction. You work in that industry and I'm looking for a good location that will attract a lot of renters. It's a big investment, I will need to make my money back."

I nod, and start eating again, going through all of the new construction that is set to close soon. The condos on 69th might work, but 74th is better. They are more upscale, but still in a manageable price range.

"Got any ideas?"

"74th would be best bang for your buck. If you put on there that it's close to all the big shopping areas, it will rent out like hot cakes."

She nods, and we finish our dinner without discussing properties any further. The food is delicious enough for me to have three helpings, leaving behind just enough for me to take home for Carleigh. She has never had my mother's cooking and she's missing out.

"What are you doing?" she asks ,while I'm filling up a Tupperware with spaghetti.

"Taking the rest for Carleigh. You don't eat leftovers."

"Who is Carleigh?"

I shut my eyes, forgetting that I never told my mom that I moved in with a girl. Now, I have no chance but to come clean.

"She's my roommate, ma. You'd like her. She makes the best pastries and even makes me homemade pizza rolls."

The gleam in her eye is astounding. "It's not like that. We are just roommates. Don't go get your hopes up."

"I mean, you seem to like her. Why can't you be more than roommates?" she says, leaning up against the counter.

"That would be weird. We live together."

I say this out loud, but in my mind I think about what it would be like to kiss her lips? I know, I know, such a douchebag. She should be comfortable around me, and not have to worry about this, but I have never mentioned it to Carleigh. My luck, she would kick me out, and then I'd have to come back here.

"Relationships have started out with friendships. Are you guys friends?"

"I think so. We don't know much about each other. We haven't been living together that long, ma."

My mother is meddling again, and usually it infuriates me, but right now I'm listening to her and she's right. Is it possible that I'm developing feelings for the girl who is way out of my league?

7

CARLEIGH

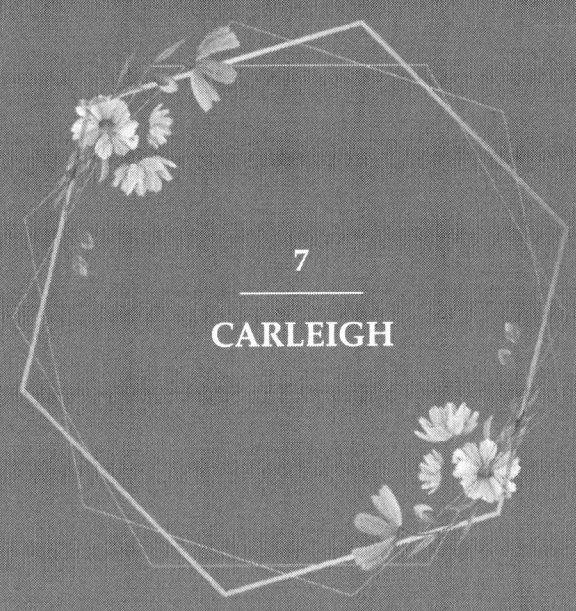

One week after Bryson's birthday, I get sick. It really doesn't come as a surprise. The signs were all there. I've been tired since Tuesday-ish, but I write that off as poor sleeping, which is sort of a persistent problem of mine anyway. On Wednesday, my pre-dinner run is sluggish and time is awful. On Thursday, my throat is like sandpaper, and by the time I finish another set of revisions and crawl into bed that evening, my legs and arms are mildly achy.

Today, I wake up with a full-blown cold.

The one silver lining is I don't have class on Fridays; it's usually a writing and research day for me at the library. The downside is I'm going to have to call in sick for work tonight at the bar, and probably tomorrow, too - which are the two days of the week where I make the best tips.

Plus, it's five-thirty in the morning, and I can't sleep in, because Bryson is singing again.

This time I'm pretty sure it's not even a real song, but

something he made up, because there are lyrics that reference sauerkraut and fishing. No way those two things would end up sharing a verse in an actual song. It's probably an annoying habit, I figure, but he's so cheerful while he does it - so quirky, genuine, and quintessentially Bryson that it's become kind of endearing.

Except now. Now I want it to stop.

So, I drag my tired, aching body out of bed and wrap the comforter around me. It's the end of May now, with the near-summer city heat just burgeoning outside, but I'm freezing in my usual t-shirt and pajama shorts. It drags on the floor behind me as I shuffle to my bedroom door, open it, and croak, "Bryson, please."

He's in the kitchen eating an egg sandwich, already dressed for work in what I recognize as his mandated t-shirt for work. Navy blue, with *Glover Construction* emblazoned on the chest. He's wearing a backward baseball cap, as he nearly always does, with a pen sticking out of the side, the purpose of which I've never really understood.

"Oops, sorry." Bryson makes an apologetic face as he notices me. "Go back to sleep, I'm almost gone."

That's certainly in my plans. But right now, since I'm awake, I should pee and find some cold meds to knock me out. "It's okay," I say, as I approach the kitchen gingerly, infusing my voice with all the energy I can muster. "I think Nyquil is in my future anyway."

His eyebrows knit together in concern. "You not feeling great?"

I shake my head. "Summer cold. To distinguish itself from my fall, winter, and spring colds, this one comes when it's nice outside." It's a bit of an exaggeration, but not really: I do get sick a lot.

Which is why, when I open the cupboard above the microwave and find my last Nyquil package empty, a sad moan sounds. "Oh no." I should be more prepared for this.

Bryson hovers over my shoulder. "You out?"

I sigh. "Yeah." I raise the heel of my palm to my forehead. I'm going to have to go up the block. "When does that bodega open, six?" I ask, mostly rhetorically.

I begin to trudge back toward the bathroom to at least take care of my bladder, then throw a favorite sweat suit on, and hopefully that'll make me feel good for enough time to make it there and back without collapsing.

Two hands halt my progress on my shoulders. "Whoa." Bryson appears in front of me. "Where ya think you're going?"

"To use the bathroom, then to go buy meds," I say, in what I'm horrified to recognize as a wheeze.

"No, no you aren't." Bryson crosses his arms over his chest. I don't even have the energy to really appreciate how good his biceps look in his shirt. "Well okay, the peeing thing you can do. But no way in hell are you going anywhere like this."

I have no energy to argue with him; he has to leave for work right away, so I'll just go as soon as he's gone. "Fine. Hold my blanket while I pee, then," I say, hoisting my heavy comforter off my body and into his hands.

I use the washroom as quickly as my tired, sore body will allow. As I wash my hands, I appraise myself for the first time in the mirror. And wow, do I ever look truly awful: my eyes are kind of red, with darkening shades of purple beneath, and my already pale skin has taken on a sickly, pallid tone. As I leave the bathroom, regret washes over me for not dumping the comforter just outside the bathroom door, because not only are goosebumps fluttering up my arms and legs, but I don't sleep in a bra and that fact is now very apparent.

I wrap my arms around myself as I exit the bathroom, feeling suddenly small and child-like. *How embarrassing.*

Bryson is waiting in the kitchen where I left him. He holds the comforter open for me when I approach, and folds it around me with his long arms as I step into it. "Here you go," he says, in a far more gentle tone than I've heard him use before. "Now come on, let's put you to bed," he adds, leading me with an arm around my shoulders toward the bedroom.

I want to inform him, *I'm a big girl and can do this part myself.* I should. But I'm so tired, and he's warm with his arm around me. Plus, he's essentially a friend now, right?

My brain must be working slower than usual, because by the time I work through this dilemma in my head, Bryson's already gotten me to lay down on the bed and is tucking the comforter around my feet. He disappears for a minute, then returns with a glass of water and a jar of what appears to be...

"Garlic," Bryson proclaims. "Lacto-fermented garlic. Eat some when you feel up to it, okay? Garlic will help. But just in case 'modern medicine' -" he punctuates this with air quotes - "has something going for it, I'm going to run to the bodega to get you some Nyquil, too."

No. "You'll be -" I wheeze - "you'll be late for work. It's okay, I can go -"

He dismisses my protest with a wave of his hand. "I've got a great record, Carleigh, Stop arguing, I'll be back in a jiffy."

Bryson disappears from my room, and one minute later, the door to our apartment opens and closes. I shut my eyes and try to focus on breathing in and out, in and out, like my favorite yoga instructor always tells me. It works pretty well up until a breath catches an itch in my throat and it turns into a hacking cough.

For someone who's sick a lot, I figure I should really be better at it by now.

A few minutes pass, and the apartment door opens again. Bryson shows up in my bedroom with two blue liquid-gel pills a moment later. "The box is above the microwave. And Dayquil for later," he assures me. "Take these."

I drag myself up on my elbows to down the medication, a process Bryson apparently has decided to supervise. I drink the rest of the water he brought earlier, and he mercifully decides to refill it before leaving.

Bryson sets it down on the bedside table beside the garlic. "Rest that pretty little head, alright?" he rambles, lifting the comforter above my shoulders. "You'll feel better in a little while. That's a Kennedy promise."

A smile appears, half into my pillow.

"I'm off around three, probably make it home by four. You need anything else, you give me a holler, alright?"

"I will," I yawn, my eyes already closed. "Thank you."

"It's nothing, Carleigh." He flicks the lights off and closes the door. If he makes it out of the apartment before I fall asleep, I don't hear it.

When I wake up just after lunchtime, the drowsiness is still there, but mostly I'm hungry. I send a quick text to my boss at the bar, since I won't be making it tonight, and will check in tomorrow. A couple of other messages were in the notification list. There's one from my mother and one from Molly, but there's two from Bryson that I open first.

It's from around 10:00 am.

Bryson: *Spicy Thai takeout for supper? Always makes me feel good when I'm all stuffed up.*

Bryson: *don't forget to eat garlic.*

I eye the garlic on my bedside table suspiciously. I'm not just going to eat a clove of garlic. That's disgusting. Maybe crush it up and use it in an omelet or something would be significantly less disgusting.

Me: *Thai sounds delicious. We can order when you get home. My treat.*

I respond to the other messages before pulling myself out of bed and shuffling to the bathroom. A hot shower, some food, then more drugs, and I'll be good as new.

It does help, but not as much as I hoped. The small burst of energy is helpful to make an egg white omelet with garlic and cilantro, brew coffee, then settle on the couch in my favorite red sweatpants and a white t-shirt that I usually reserve for baking days. It's comfortable and actually fits pretty nicely, with short sleeves and the words but *first, coffee* on the front, but it got stained irreparably with olive oil last year, so it's been banished from public view.

I'm halfway through an episode of *The Real Housewives of Atlanta* when my phone buzzes. It's him, replying to the proof-of-life picture I sent him of crushed garlic.

Bryson: *That's the stuff... you feeling any better?*
Me: *A bit after sleep and food, thanks to you!*

I move to set the phone aside, but on a whim, I snatch it back.

Me: *How's work today? Did you get in trouble for being late?*

Bryson: *No. Who could get mad at this face?*

There's probably some truth to that. How should I respond? I don't, but instead slide my phone onto the coffee table and drop my head to the arm of the couch. I may have slept all morning, but my eyelids still feel a little heavy, so I give up and let myself take an afternoon nap.

When my eyes open next, it's after four. I can't see Bryson, but the water is running in the bathroom, so he must be home. I sit up on my elbow and grab my phone off the table.

Mom: *How you feeling?*

As I tap out a reply, the water turns off, then a few minutes later, the door to the bathroom creaks open.

Bryson is humming to himself down the hallway. I should really get up and do something productive; he's had a full day of work and I've been just laying here like a sloth. Sickness or not, that's not like me. Heck, I didn't even wash the plate from my omelet.

That realization is enough to get my feet on the floor. I make my way to the kitchen and reach into the sink for my plate, but it's empty.

"Bryson," I mutter.

"Yes?" He appears at my side suddenly, sliding in like Cosmo Kramer. "You rang?"

I turn toward him, one hand on my hip. "You washed my plate!"

He tilts his head curiously. "Was I not supposed to?"

"I was going to do it. You didn't have to."

Bryson shrugs. "No big deal. You're sick." He reaches out and places a large palm on my forehead. "How you feeling, anyways? Your head don't feel hot."

"I think I feel okay." I take a brief self-assessment; my headache has subsided and my body isn't as tired as it was earlier, but my throat still feels pretty scratchy. "Definitely can't go to work tonight, though. It's a pity."

"Think of it as a free Friday off!" Bryson exclaims, clapping his hands together. He strides out of the kitchen and into the living room, where he plops down somewhat unceremoniously on one end of the sofa. "Nothing wrong with taking it easy."

I get myself a glass of water and then follow, sitting gently down on the other end where I left my pile of blankets. "Normally I'd agree," I reply, which is kind of a lie. I've always been bad at relaxation. "But Friday and Saturday are my good tip nights. Maybe I can pick up a shift next Wednesday for wing night to try and make up for it."

"That's the spirit." He claps his hand on his knee. "You get in there and bat them eyelashes of yours and sell those wings!"

I chuckle. "Fifty-cent wings sell themselves."

Bryson's eyes widen. "Great deal. Where's this place again?"

"Logan's, it's in the Financial District not far from the Trade Center. Little dive sort of place, but it gets a decent crowd on weekends. Post-work drinks are pretty popular too, but I usually don't work too much of that."

"You don't want them greasy stock trader types all over

you anyway." Bryson waves his hand. "I bet they tip good, though."

I smile at him and reach for the remote; the *Real Housewives* has been stalled at "next episode?" on the TV for god knows how long now. "Not all of them. Depends if there are girls around they want to impress with their hundred-dollar bills."

"Wrong kind of guy."

"Wrong kind of girl, too. But it's not all that type - Logan's is pretty casual for them." I hand Bryson the remote. "I've been laying here all day, it's yours if you want it." I assume he'll be heading out later; he's usually got some kind of social engagement going on, and seems to be a popular guy, which I understand now. Bryson's fun to be around and he's not a total asshole.

He refuses my offer of the remote. "No, no. You're sick, you get to pick. Those are the rules, Carleigh."

I giggle. "According to whom?"

"Everyone."

"I can watch more embarrassing reality TV when you're out later."

He quirks an eyebrow at me. "Who says I'm going out later?"

"Er." I can feel my cheeks flush inexplicably. "I kind of just assumed. You're usually out on weekends, aren't you?"

"Yeah, but you're sick." Bryson reaches out and taps the ball of one of my feet, which has edged its way out from beneath the blanket. "I've got to keep you company."

"Oh." I give him a little smile. "You don't have to take pity on me, it's okay. Kandi and Porsha will keep me company." At his blank look, I point toward the TV. "Housewives."

"Oh." Bryson rolls his eyes. "Fine, let me rephrase - I want to keep you company. If that's alright."

"Of course, you live here, too." I nibble on my lower lip, secretly glad he's not leaving. It's sort of nice, just hanging out. Maybe I've been lonelier than I thought since Trinity left. I decide to make more of an effort to see Molly and my other friends. "If you're sticking around, do you want to watch a movie tonight, maybe?"

"That sounds great," Bryson says enthusiastically. "What are you in the - oh, I know. Let's watch Mission Impossible! Actually, let's watch the second one, that's the best one."

His suggestion actually sounds pretty good to me; I've already seen all of the movies, so if I fall asleep, I won't be missing anything, but they're also entertaining enough that I might stay awake.

"Good idea," I reply. "But first let's order food."

∼

"ETHAN HUNT IS SO COOL," Bryson says an hour later, two chopsticks full of noodles half to his mouth. "Just hanging off that mountain like it's nothing."

I look over at him. He always seems excited, but particularly right now; his blue eyes are lit up, his grin wide enough I can see the slight gap in his teeth on one side. "If you were a secret agent, I bet you could do that too."

Bryson shakes his head. "No way, Carleigh. I don't like heights."

I laugh. "I don't think you'd be afraid of heights if you were Ethan Hunt."

"Hey." He points a finger at me accusingly. "I'm not afraid of heights, bud. I just don't like them."

I grin and quirk my head. "Is there a difference?"

"You bet your ass there is. Now come on, quiet on set." Bryson nudges my knee with his knuckles. "He's getting a secret message."

I smile at the irony of him telling someone to be quiet - he's probably the loudest person I've ever met - but I obey. I lean back on the couch, a container of spicy noodles in my blanket-covered lap, and continue to eat quietly.

I haven't eaten a lot today, but I'm still not feeling great. So, I set the half-empty container down on the table, curl my feet beneath me, and tug the blanket to my chin.

A little while later, Bryson finishes his own noodles and peers into my takeout box. "That all you're eating?"

"Yeah, I'm full. I'd tell you to eat my leftovers if you want, but you'll probably get sick."

"You've been breathing on me all evening. If I'm going to get sick it's going to happen anyway. But nah, I'll put them in the fridge. You need the noodle energy to get better!" Bryson stands up and begins to clear the takeout containers.

I look up at him with a smile. "The noodle energy?"

Bryson raises his eyebrows very seriously. "Yeah, Carleigh. The noodle energy."

"Okay, Bryson." I turn my gaze back to the TV, but the corners of my lips don't drop. "I don't know where you get some of that from."

"Some of what?" he calls from the kitchen. There's a slight clanging noise that I recognize as cutlery hitting the steel of the sink, probably having fallen from the drying rack. "Oh, sorry bud," I hear him apologize. "Back in here you go."

"Your ... Bryson-isms," I reply, tugging my blanket out of his way as he walks back into the living room. "Noodle energy. The garlic thing. You know, Bryson-isms."

He drops his large frame back onto the couch. A little closer to me this time, I can't help but notice. "This head's a wild place to be," he says, tapping his ear. "But the garlic thing is just common sense! Everybody knows that!"

"I'm not sure that's true," I laugh, "but okay."

"You doubt me now, but when you wake up tomorrow feeling right as rain, you'll be a believer," he informs me. "Now you going to share this blanket or what?"

It's warmer under the soft polyester with him. Part of that is probably because I scooted a bit closer, but in general, he seems to be radiating heat. As someone who is usually too cold, I'm jealous.

"You're cold?" Bryson says, sounding alarmed. "Well come here, then." He lifts an arm up, gesturing with his hand for mine to move beneath it. "Heater at your service, if you want."

This feels like it's crossing some kind of line, but absolutely everything I know about Bryson tells me this is nothing more than another genuinely kind gesture. I tuck myself in closer, let his arm drape over my shoulders, and honestly, it feels pretty nice. He's warm and comfy despite the thick muscle I know is there beneath his soft t-shirt, and large enough that I feel pretty enveloped by the whole experience.

"You really are a heater," I say, resting my hands awkwardly on my lap.

"Yes!" he replies cheerfully, rubbing his palm on my goosebump-ridden bicep. "Jesus, your skin's freezing, Maybe you should go see a doctor."

"It's just a cold, Bryson, I'm not dying." I lift the blanket a bit higher. He takes the hint and tugs the edge of it over my shoulder, then slides his arm down behind my back. I shift slightly to get comfortable, my right shoulder now leaning against his chest instead of beneath his arm. I'm also facing fully and mercifully away from him now, and hopefully he can't see how red my face is right now.

Pathetic. I can't believe it's really been that long since I've done so much as cuddle with a man, even platonically like this, that the simple touch of Bryson's hand near my hip makes me blush. It has been about a year since I broke up with my last boyfriend, and at least six months since I've been on a real date.

"This is why you need the noodle energy," Bryson says matter-of-factly.

"I'm still not following."

He squeezes my waist, then lets his big hand rest there, wrapped around my side. *It's fine, completely fine.* "There's nothing to you. More noodles, more energy, then boom! More heat."

His statement is pretty untrue. There's plenty to me. I've never been a naturally slender person, the type that could eat anything and not gain weight. On the contrary, I'm pretty acutely aware of the impact of every thousand calories. Not overweight by any means, but that's probably just because of the whole marathon training thing and my own valiant attempts to eat more healthily.

I swallow, close my eyes briefly, and make an executive

decision to just get out of my own head. I'm going to enjoy this dumb action movie and the big, comfortable goof who is nice enough to sit with me during it. "I'll take that under advisement, Dr. Kennedy," I say dryly.

The scene turns suddenly dark, and in the reflection of the TV, I can see him grin.

8

BRYSON

I really, truly didn't plan it, but when Quinn asks me to meet for a drink and requests somewhere in lower Manhattan, I suggest Logan's even before I remember Carleigh works tonight.

I text Quinn on the way to the subway.

Bryson: *They've got fifty cent wings on Wednesdays. My roommate works there.*

My phone buzzes just as I'm at the bottom of the stairs underground.

Quinn: *Ah the mysterious new roommate! Does this mean I get to meet her?*

Bryson: *I'm not sure if she's working tonight.*

I shove my phone in my pocket and spend the next ten minutes on the train wondering why I bother lying. Carleigh's my friend. It's not weird to grab a drink at the place your friend works. It's not like I picked it because she works there – they have cheap wings! – but it's certainly not a drawback.

She's not at home when I get there. She's probably still at school or the library or a coffee shop or wherever she goes during the day, since she doesn't usually leave for work until a bit later. I grab a shower, change, and then head back out to meet my friend.

He sends me a text when I'm only a block away.

Quinn: *I grabbed a table by the bar. To the left when you walk in.*

I don't respond; by the time I'm finished reading Quinn's message, I'm basically outside the door. Logan's is clearly a dive, not in the sort of intentional way all those bullshit hipster places have adopted, but it looks decent enough.

The crowd inside is a mix of guys in crisp pressed shirts, Patagonia vests, and girls in ironed pencil skirts. I spot Quinn right away; he's always wearing an expensive version of old, shitty clothes, and he fits in pretty well with the try-hard groups in the bar. I've told him a bunch of times he looks like a jackass wearing a one-hundred dollar pre-torn shirt, but we're old friends and I love the guy, even if he is a jackass.

"Hey bud," I greet, folding my oversized frame onto a bar-height stool and leaning over the small, rounded wooden table. "What's up?"

"Just got here," Quinn says. He nods behind him, toward the bar. "We got a hot waitress. Dark hair, tight shirt. With the ponytail."

Oh no. My eyes fall behind him, to where Quinn referenced, and – yep. It's Carleigh, dressed in jeans, a faded green t-shirt, and a half-apron emblazoned with the bar's name tied at her hips. She's at the bar gathering a tray full of golden-colored beers and is thankfully far enough away to not have heard my buddy talking.

"Er." I wince slightly. "So, that's Carleigh, actually."

Quinn's eyebrows shoot up. "Oh, oops. Sorry. She is hot, though."

"Yeah, yeah." I'm not denying this. She looks especially cute today, with the slim cut of her jeans and that shirt doing absolutely nothing to hide the curves I recently got a little closer with. She'd been sick – thus a bit more willing to accept help than usual – and in attempting to make her feel better I somehow ended up cuddling with her on the couch. I'm definitely not still thinking about how the turn of her waist felt under my hands.

Carleigh walks back toward us, stopping to drop off a couple of beers at a neighboring table before she turns to set what I assume is Quinn's beer in front of him. As she does, her eyes fall on me, and she makes a surprised face. "Oh! Bryson!"

I grin at her. "Hi. Figured we'd come get some of them cheap wings you were talking about. This is my buddy, Quinn."

He reaches his hand out to shake hers. "Jackson Quinn," he introduces. "Nice to meet you."

Carleigh takes it. "Nice to meet you, too," she replies, with a quick smile before looking back at me. Her eyes meet mine and then quickly drop to her now-empty tray before flicking back up at me. She seems shy suddenly, uneasy, and I hope I didn't make her uncomfortable by coming here. Her weight shifts to one foot, then she says, "So, what can I get for you?"

"Dealer's choice. Nothing too dark, though, it isn't winter anymore."

She smiles and nods. "I'll make an executive decision."

"I trust ya, you've got good taste. After all, you picked me as your roommate!"

"I think that actually shows she's got bad taste," Quinn cuts in, teasing.

I put a faux-offended look on my face. "Oh, come on."

Carleigh laughs at Quinn. "He came recommended from a trustworthy friend, so it was more about my faith in Evan's judgment than anything," she responds. Then she pats my knee, which is sticking out half-into the aisle – the world is truly just not made for tall people – and adds, "But he's more than proved himself. There are so many jars I don't have to struggle to open anymore."

I chuckle, remembering the jar of miso that she'd asked me to open just the day before. "You should really work on your grip strength," I advise.

"What for? I've got you around now." There's a new lightness in Carleigh's expression when she meets my eyes, the sense of awkwardness gone. "I'll be back with something for you. You guys want a wing menu, too?"

Quinn nods. "Absolutely," he answers, then she walks away. He turns to look over his shoulder, and once she's a few tables away, he looks back and says, "Dude, you're so into her."

"What? Carleigh? No." Quinn's eyebrows raise again, and I shake my head. "Not everything has to be like that."

"I agree, not everything has to, but this definitely is." Quinn takes a long sip from his beer. "I've known you for a thousand years, Kennedy. I know that look."

I scoff. "Piss off."

Quinn shrugs. "Fine. So, you don't mind if I ask her out, then?"

I glare at him remembering why I hate old friends. They're the worst. They know you too well and they're impossible to hide from.

"I knew it," Quinn says gleefully. "Don't worry, I'm hands off. Since you're clearly hands on-"

"I swear, Quinn, I'm going to rip your throat out."

"Very mid-2000s Rambo of you, but you're definitely too weak for that."

"Oh screw that, I'm definitely strong enough! You want to go outside and try, bud?" I challenge, the threat neutralized by the laughter I'm speaking through.

Quinn grins at me again, a mischievous look in his eye. "You've been trying for years to get a rematch from that time I kicked your ass at your mom's."

"That was in elementary school, bud! No way would it go that way today."

"Meet you by the flagpole after school, I guess."

I laugh, but can't think of what to reply. Right when I come up with a good response, Carleigh reappears carrying two laminated menus and a beer.

"Amber ale, local brew," she announces, tossing down a paper coaster and then setting the already-sweating glass in front of me. "And two menus. I'll give you guys a couple minutes and be right back."

"Thanks." I watch her walk to another table, her hands in the pockets of the apron, before finally looking at the menu. There are a lot of flavors, but I'm a simple guy. All I need is an order of the salt and pepper, and probably the mango habanero. Though, there's a flavor with a stupid name that has sumac and oregano in it, and another that's got kimchi in the actual name. "Quinn, what are you getting?"

He doesn't reply right away, so I look up from the menu. He's just sitting there, grinning at me. "You're gone," he teases.

I look over at Carleigh again, so Quinn probably has a point. Not that I'll ever admit it to him. She's taking an order from a table filled with guys in wannabe suits, but ever the professional, she's still got a smile on her face. One of the guys beckons her to come closer, a finger pointing up at the speaker and then at his ear. I squint, trying to read lips – it always seems to me like I should be able to do that pretty easily, but it never works out that well – there's something about noise, then the guy lifts his menu. Carleigh leans over to speak to him. A disgusting feeling arises when the guy is staring down the neckline of her shirt.

One of the guys is speaking again. I strain to hear, and manage to catch something about a lager and then, sure enough, a request for her phone number. From where I'm sitting, about half of her face is visible, which is wearing a strained, polite smile I know isn't genuine. Her reply to the guy is too quiet for me to hear, but a second later, the guy reaches out and wraps a hand around her small wrist.

My body tenses, not sure what to do. I don't want to go roaring in like a white knight – I know Carleigh well enough to get the feeling she's not any kind of damsel in distress – but at the same time, I really hate the uncomfortable expression on her face, and want to help. But before I must make a decision on how to do that, she's already extricated herself and is backing away, tucking her hands in her apron again. I try to catch her eye when she passes by our table, heading to the back, but fail.

Quinn doesn't seem to have noticed anything with his face buried in the menu when I turn back. "You think they make their own buffalo sauce?" he asks.

"Er, I don't know," I answer, distracted. "You know, I'll go ask Carleigh."

"What? No, I don't need to know that badly." Quinn replies, but I'm already out of my seat. "Oh hell, whatever."

I ignore Quinn and follow Carleigh's path toward the bar. I linger sort of awkwardly outside the door to the kitchen, ignoring the annoyed look the bartender is giving me. Mercifully, she reappears after a couple of minutes, pushing her way out of the kitchen with her shoulder. I try to read her face, but it's excessively neutral, her eyes as dark as ever.

She jumps when she sees me. "What're you doing over here? You need something?" she asks.

"Quinn had a question about the buffalo sauce," I blurt loudly. In a much gentler tone, I add, "And I saw that guy grab you, I wanted to make sure you're okay."

Carleigh's face softens, her mouth almost pouting. "Oh," she breathes, shaking her head. "I'm fine."

"You sure?"

She nods and gives me a reassuring smile. "I'm sure. You get used to dealing with it."

I make a face. "That doesn't make it any better."

Carleigh reaches up and takes my hand. "You're very sweet," she says, squeezing it. "But we have great bouncers and I promise it's fine."

I sigh and squeeze her hand back. "Okay, but if you need some asses kicked, you just give me a yell."

She nods, now clearly just humoring me, and drops my hand. "I will. Now, what's the thing with the buffalo sauce?"

"Er." I rack my brain, trying to remember. "Oh. Quinn wants to know if it's made in-house."

Carleigh gives me an odd look. "Of course. I'll bring him a little taster cup." She turns, not waiting for a reply, and goes back into the kitchen.

When I get back to the table, Quinn seems to have made a decision. "I'm getting three kinds," he announces.

"Great," I reply, still distracted. "Which ones?"

Usually, when I meet Quinn or any of the other guys for a drink after work, we hop around to a few different places, but today Quinn doesn't suggest leaving. He might be annoying, but he's a great friend where it counts. Quinn catches me up on his new job as an events promoter, we talk about our friend Andrew, who recently followed his girlfriend to California, we argue about the Rangers – and eventually, Quinn stops shooting teasing looks at me whenever my attention falls to Carleigh.

It happens a lot.

I don't want to think too hard about the sudden protectiveness I feel toward Carleigh. I'm attracted to her, that's all; it's a physical thing, which I can't help. Plus, she's my friend, and I want my friends to feel happy and safe and all that good shit. It's definitely got nothing to do with any actual feelings, or anything. Definitely not. I really should try to cool it and not glance over every ten minutes. Really. I should try.

Besides, Carleigh can obviously take care of herself. I

know the table of guys from earlier are definitely not the only people in the bar who have hit on her tonight, though none of them I see after, seem to physically impose on her. She handles them all with a practiced ease, and I'm reminded of the fact she's worked here since long before I knew her, and she didn't need a babysitter.

I still kind of want to be back on the couch with my arms around her, keeping her safe, but I fight the urge. I can learn to evolve.

Around eight, the crowd dies down a little. I'm kind of surprised until I remember that we're in the Financial District, which can be kind of dead once the time for after work drinks or dinner is through, especially on a Wednesday. Carleigh comes to our table with a sheepish smile and her hands in her apron.

"Hey, it's slowing down, so I'm getting sent home early, since I'm just covering a shift," she explains. "Do you guys mind if I settle up with you? You can start a new tab with Teresa, she'll be taking over."

"Sure, Carleigh," I say immediately. "No problem."

Quinn pulls out his wallet. "Big plans for the rest of the night?"

I smile at that; I imagine her night will have something to do with a reality show, a blanket, and maybe a glass of Lillet.

"No big plans, unless you count watching *Below Deck*," Carleigh answers, taking Quinn's credit card.

"You're really predictable, Murphy, you know that?"

Carleigh rolls her eyes at me. "Give me your credit card."

"Now Carleigh, is that any way to get a good tip?" I tease, handing her my card.

"Careful," she warns with a wink, "I know where you sleep."

I grin at her. "Threats, Carleigh? You wound me."

"Why don't you join us?" Quinn interrupts. "Have a drink."

Carleigh hesitates, like she's trying to turn down the offer, but in a friendly way. I'm about to jump in with an easy out for her, but she replies before I can speak.

"If you guys want to go somewhere else, then sure," she says, to my surprise. "But I really don't want to hang around work anymore."

"Sure, we can go somewhere else," Quinn agrees. "There are a few places on the next block."

Carleigh gives me a closed-mouth smile, her shoulders a little tense. "Great." She meets my eyes; I grin at her cheerfully, and she relaxes. "I'll go run these," she says, holding up our cards, then leaves.

Once we're settled up, Quinn and I wait outside. The air has gotten a little chillier, but it's still June in New York, and I don't think it will be cold for months. Quinn's got his cell phone out and is talking to god-knows-who – he's got a more involved social life than I could ever want – so it's only me paying attention when Carleigh walks out of Logan's. She's ditched the apron in favor of a purse slung across her shoulders, and her hair is down now.

"Hey," I greet quietly, taking a few steps away from Quinn. "I just wanted to apologize for earlier – you can take care of yourself, Carleigh, and I know that. I realized after it seemed like maybe I thought you couldn't, and I'm not trying to insinuate anything."

Carleigh seems caught off guard by the apology, but after

a couple of seconds, she just shakes her head and smiles at me. "Oh, Bryson," she says, touching my elbow. "It was really nice of you to check in. Everything was fine, but it means a lot to me you cared enough to ask. Now, are you going to buy me a drink, or what?"

"Am I going to buy you a drink?" I exclaim, feigning shock. "Babe, I just gave you a twenty-five percent tip. I should be asking you that."

"I'll make you cheese bread on Saturday," she bargains.

I frown at her. "I saw you get groceries yesterday. I know you were going to make that anyway. But yeah, yeah, okay, can't say no to you." Quinn, still on the phone, beckons for us to follow him. I sling an arm around Carleigh's shoulders and duck my head conspiratorially. "If we play our cards right, maybe Hollywood over there'll buy us both drinks."

Carleigh laughs. As we walk down the street, I'm pretty sure she leans into me a little.

One hour and nine ounces of wine later, Carleigh is leaning into me a lot.

We're crowded into a curved half-booth at a hipster bar not far from Logan's. The booth is really not meant for tall people, let alone two of them, and Carleigh's leg pressed up beside mine since the start. As she nurses a big glass of wine, though, the rest of her begins melting toward me too.

I'm probably encouraging it, honestly. Quinn started telling her a story about when we'd gotten in shit for trying to help our grounded friend break out of his own house, a story that really makes me look pretty ridiculous, and when she turned to me in a fit of giggles, I tickle her side a little to retaliate. She squirms around and almost falls out of the tall booth, so I grab her, haul her back in, and then never move my arm from behind her shoulders. *It's more comfortable this way anyway without my big arm in the way*, I figure. It definitely has nothing to do with how Carleigh immediately takes that opportunity to melt into my side.

The air conditioning in the bar is a little crazy, I reason.

"Hey," Carleigh says suddenly. "If I order fried pickles, will you guys help me eat them?"

"Is the Pope Catholic, Carleigh?" I joke. "Obviously!"

"Great." She slides out from my side – I try hard not to notice it now feels kind of cold – and meanders off to the bar to place the order.

Quinn smiles at me. "I like her for you, man."

I scoff. "Not this again. Quinn -"

"Just saying." He jerks his head in Carleigh's general direction. "She seems to like you. She's even laughing at your terrible jokes."

"Even if there was something, which there isn't," I emphasize, shooting a look at him, "she'd be way out of my league."

Quinn shrugs that off. "I'm telling you. She likes you." He taps his temple. "Uncle Jackson knows."

"I'm six months older than you, Uncle Jackson."

"Don't have to be older to be wiser."

"Oh, piss right off -"

Carleigh skips back in suddenly. I hope she didn't hear any of that. Judging by the gleeful look on her face, we're safe.

"What are you so happy about there?" I ask.

"Pickles are on their way," she says happily. Her cheeks are a little pink from the wine, and it's so goddamn cute, I can't stop myself from laughing.

"Easy to please, are you?" I tease.

Quinn finishes off the last of his pint. "Everyone loves pickles, Bryson. I'm going to get another, you guys need any?"

I hold up my half-empty pint and nod, but Carleigh shakes her head. "I don't drink that much, I need to wait it out."

"Alright." With a nod, Quinn disappears into the crowd.

"You guys are funny together," Carleigh observes, tapping her fingernail on the base of her wine glass. "Your accent is thicker than his, though. Why's that?"

I point at myself. "I haven't got an accent, that's the rest of you." Carleigh rolls her eyes at me, and I laugh. "Yeah, yeah. Probably because Quinn spends half his time trying to impress girls in Manhattan and most of them socialite types don't want a guy that talks like he works in a boat yard in Jersey."

"Those girls are all boring anyway," Carleigh says, waving her hand. "If I had to pick between the two of you, I'd pick you any day, Bryson."

It's pathetic just how much that warms my heart. "Thanks," I say sincerely, squeezing her knee in thanks. "Nice of you to say."

Carleigh grabs my hand just before I can withdraw it from her leg. "I mean it," she insists.

I take a chance and spread my palm across her thigh. She sighs, sounding content, and relaxes into me again. "I can't wait for my pickles."

9

CARLEIGH

I'm pretty sure that we are friends. I've met one of his friends, Quinn, and we've all hung out a couple of times. My best friend, Molly, has been around the apartment and met Bryson as well, and in general, it feels like we've become regular parts of each other's lives.

Despite that, I'm not expecting it when he invites me to New Jersey to celebrate the Fourth of July.

I usually go to my parents' house at the Cape for the fourth, but this year they are in France, my sister has other plans, and there's something about being in the empty house up there by myself that seems less than ideal. I have tentative replacement plans to do something with Molly, but we haven't actually settled on anything specific. I assume we'll be drinking wine and light cocktails in my apartment all night, which sounds just fine to me. Bryson's invite comes while I'm making dinner on the second night, right after he asks me when I'm leaving for Massachusetts.

"Oh, if you aren't going up to the Cape, you must come to Jersey with us!"

It seems like a pity invite so I decline.

"Oh no, it's okay." I spill a container of grape tomatoes onto the counter and begin slicing them in half for easier addition into the salad I'm building.

Bryson stands up and moves beside me, resting his elbows on the countertop to my right. He pops a stray tomato in his mouth. "It'll be a lot of fun. We're going to have a barbecue at Quinn's, then there's the fireworks and shit at Exchange Place at night. Plus drinks all day, obviously. Just celebrating the good ol' U-S-of-A! You can't stay here by yourself."

It does sound like fun, but it also sounds like a long day of social interaction for somebody who considers themselves to be a pretty heavy introvert. "I won't be alone, Bryson, don't worry. I'm supposed to be doing something with Molly."

"Something other than Lillet and *Real Housewives*?"

I glare at him. "Maybe *Below Deck*."

Bryson laughs easily, his whole body contracting and releasing, mirth in his blue eyes. "Come on. Bring Molly. She'll have a great time. You both will! I promise. At least ask her!"

I hesitate. "I'll check with her," I relent. "But if she's not into the idea -"

"She will be," he cuts in confidently. "Who wouldn't want to spend July 4th in God's country?"

I laugh as I bring up Molly's contact information on my phone. "Is that what we're calling Jersey now?"

"Hey, I won't settle for any of that slander, Murphy."

Bryson stands up straight and knocks his hip into mine. "Move over, I'll finish chopping."

My eyes fall to his hands as he begins slicing tomatoes. They move quickly, almost expertly; I wonder where he learned to handle a knife that well. He's killed things in the woods and then cooked them over a fire, or something.

Molly answers on the second ring. "Carleigh!"

"Hey. I was just calling about - hang on." Bryson is nudging me with his elbow. "What?"

"Put it on speaker!" he suggests happily.

He's got a big smile on his face that's really hard to say no to, so I oblige. "Okay, you're on speaker because Bryson -"

"Hi, Molly!" Bryson calls out loudly.

"Jesus, she's on the phone, not in Timbuktu."

"Sorry, sorry. Hi, Molly," he repeats, his voice softer.

A laugh comes over the line. "Hi."

"Bryson has decided that our July 4th plans of hanging out at the apartment are a little sad, so he's invited us to go to New Jersey to spend the holiday with his friends. If we're interested. I said no, but he bullied me into phoning you to ask."

"There was no bullying," Bryson insists, setting the knife down. He slides the chopped tomatoes into a dish and wipes his hands on his jeans. "I merely suggested."

"Hmm." I smile down at my phone, glad it's not FaceTime. Molly already has some ludicrous ideas about me having some kind of non-platonic feelings for my roommate - ideas that I don't want to encourage. Even if it were true, nothing good can come from acknowledging it; I'm one hundred percent not Bryson's type. There's no point in setting myself up for failure. Plus, we seem to make good friends.

"Jersey, huh?"

Bryson claps his hands. "Molly, it's going to be so fun, we'll have a barbecue and the fireworks and drinks, the whole nine yards. I'm not going to force you, but I think you and Carleigh should come and have a good time with us."

"Hm." I can hear the amusement in Molly's voice, and know immediately what her response is going to be. I also know that Molly's going to make Bryson work for it a little.

"Hmm yes, or hmm no thanks?" Bryson presses.

"Few follow up questions. When's the last ferry out of Jersey City to Manhattan? Or, do you have a place for us to sleep? Carleigh and I are ladies accustomed to a certain lifestyle, you know."

Bryson laughs. "Paulus Hook stops running around nine on holidays, I think, but you can get downtown from Harborside 'til about 11:30. But all of us usually crash at my buddy's Quinn's parents' house - they've got a pretty big place and they're normally out of town for the fourth, so they let us have the run of it. If you're alright sharing, you guys definitely will be sleeping in a bed." Bryson catches my eye and winks. I bite my lip and smile back. "That meet your approval, Miss Molly?"

"I suppose," Molly says slowly. "One more question: will there be beer pong, and if so, will there be anyone there who's up to the challenge of playing me?"

When she says yes, I shudder. How am I going to spend an evening surrounded by people, drinking, and keep myself from staring at Bryson. This is not a good idea.

"Weak," I say accusingly, as I stalk around my bedroom, searching for the sunscreen that I know is here somewhere. "You're weak. One mention of a good time, and you sell us out for a night in New Jersey."

Molly beams at me from where she's sitting, cross-legged, atop my mattress. Her overnight bag sits on the floor near the door with a floppy hat resting on top. I, however, am not done packing, because I got sidetracked proofreading an email to send to a professor and ended up redrafting part of the paper I was asking him to read, and now I can't find my damn sunscreen.

"Oh come on, it'll be fun. You knew we were going the second you phoned me."

Okay, that's mostly true. "Not my fault Bryson's persuasive."

Molly cocks her head to the side, looking not unlike a curious Golden Retriever. "Oh, are you finding it hard to resist those baby blues?"

I throw a rejected tank top at her. "Shut up. None of that, okay? We're friends."

"Carleigh, he looks at you like you're made of like … moonlight."

"He looks at everyone like that." I open my top drawer for the fourth time, digging around again, and then finally - "Success! Found it."

"Great." Molly shuffles to the end of the bed and grabs my backpack, zipping it open. "Now come on, throw it in here, and - why do you have running shoes in here?" Molly digs in a bit deeper. "And a sports bra, and shorts, and - it's the fourth of July."

I glare at her and snatch the bag away, shoving everything back in. "And my training schedule says I have to run twelve miles tomorrow. If I wait until we're back in the city, it'll be too hot. So, I'll have to do it in the morning."

"You're crazy," Molly declares, but doesn't argue. She slides off the bed, grabs her own bag, then opens my bedroom door. "We're ready!"

Bryson is waiting in the kitchen near the entranceway, prodding at one of the new entries at the fermentation station. "Oh hey, only twenty-minutes late!" he says, pointing at the clock on the microwave. "Not too bad for Carleigh."

"Hey," I object weakly, but even I know it's a futile protest. I do have a bit of a punctuality problem. But I'm working on it. Kind of.

"Aw come on, I'm just teasing." Bryson reaches out and squeezes my shoulder, then opens the apartment door and holds it for us. "Let's go, ladies, we haven't got all day." He flashes a goofy grin at me as I pass by. "Might have to fit in some autograph time, actually. People on the ferry are going to think I'm a big deal, showing up with you two!"

I roll my eyes affectionately at him and intentionally ignore Molly's pointed smirk. I slip my other arm through my backpack straps and hoist it comfortably onto my shoulders, then lead the way through the hallway, down the stairs and onto the street.

∼

THREE HOURS LATER, I have to admit that I'm having a pretty good time, sitting on the edge of a red brick step with a bottle of cherry kombucha in my hand. My back to the door of the house we're staying in, talking to a girl named Sawyer, who is apparently one of Bryson's friends from high school. Nearby, there's a raucous game of beer pong going, and just past that, a game of ladder golf. It's a pretty spacious yard, at least for Jersey City, but something tells me this group of people would find a way to have a good time even if there wasn't a backyard at all.

I've met a lot of different people since showing up with Molly and Bryson a couple of hours earlier, but I only remember a few names: Quinn, obviously, who I've met before and whose parents' house they've apparently commandeered, Sawyer, and Max. They've been nice and welcoming, and mercifully only a few of them seem to be on Bryson's level of positive chaos.

"So, you're from Massachusetts, I think Bryson said?" Sawyer asks. "How do you like New York?"

"Missouri, actually," I say. "I grew up in St. Louis. I went to school in Massachusetts, though."

Sawyer smiles. "Bryson told us you did your undergrad at Harvard."

"Oh, I - yeah," I confirm, feeling a brief flush of heat in my cheeks. "I moved to New York a couple of years ago for grad school, and I love it. It's probably my favorite city in the world. Never a dull moment."

"Especially, now that you've got Bryson as your roommate, I bet," Sawyer jokes. "You must have the patience of a saint. I love Bryson, he's the nicest guy around, but I can't imagine he's easy to live with."

As if on cue, Bryson chooses that moment to amble away from the ladder golf setup, where he'd been engaged in active commentary of a seemingly contentious game between two guys named Royce and Bishop. "Hey, I heard my name, Krishna!" he hollers, as he strides up. "Don't be telling her lies about me!"

Sawyer holds up one hand innocently; the other is clutching a White Claw. "You're right, I shouldn't lie. He's actually not a nice guy at all."

"Me?" Bryson exclaims, bringing his hands to his chest. "I'm the salt of the earth! Right Quinn?"

Quinn, who's been engrossed in conversation with Molly near the beer pong table for at least twenty-minutes now, barely looks up. "That's right, bud!"

I laugh. "Only good things, I swear."

Sawyer hesitates. "Well, in the interests of honesty, I did just presume that you were probably difficult to live with."

"Oh!" Bryson raises his eyebrows. "And what'd she say?"

"She didn't answer yet."

Bryson crouches down in front of me and rests his elbow on his knee. He drops his chin into his hand, letting a beer dangle from his fingers, and says, "Well, Carleigh? Am I difficult to live with?"

I laugh and glances down at my pale knees, then back up, not quite making eye contact. "He's a great roommate," I tell Sawyer truthfully. "He fixed the sink the other day."

"See!" Bryson vaults to his feet. "Knew I'd come in handy, didn't you, Carleigh?"

"Yes. I haven't needed to use the step stool in weeks."

Sawyer chuckles and downs the rest of her drink. "Well, I need another. You want anything, Carleigh?"

"Oh, no thank you. I've still got most of this left." I hold up the kombucha in my hand. Then, feeling compelled as always to explain my sobriety, I add, "I'm not really much of a drinker, so I'm pacing myself until later." I don't add that one of the last times I drank around Bryson and Quinn, I ended up making an ass out of myself by hanging off of Bryson all night. He'd been nice about it, but I don't want to make it a pattern with a guy who's just my friend.

Sawyer doesn't skip a beat. "Alright, well, I'll be back! Don't let Bryson rope you into playing ladder golf with him. He says he's bad, but he's actually the best here."

Bryson grins down at me. "She isn't lying, I'm the king." Once Sawyer vacates her spot, he turns and plops down beside me. "So, having fun?"

"Yeah, I am! Everybody's really nice. You were right, Bryson. Thanks for inviting us."

"Anytime!" Bryson claps his hand down on his knee enthusiastically, then rises to his feet. "Now, come on. Sawyer probably warded you off ladder golf, but I promise I'm pretty bad at beer pong if you want to go lose to Quinn and Molly together. You can play with the 'booch if you want, I'll drink your shares." He holds his hand out, offering it to me.

I'm also terrible at beer pong, but Bryson's face is beaming hopefully at me like sunshine and roses. Plus, I'm probably the most sober person here. Maybe I'll be able to use that to my advantage and narrow Molly's margin of victory. So I agree, taking his hand.

Bryson pulls me easily to my feet. His hand drops from mine as soon as I'm standing, but then it's big, warm and flat against my lower back as he guides me toward where Molly and Quinn are standing by the beer pong table.

"Quinn," Bryson growls faux-menacingly. "You guys want to play?"

Molly smiles at me, a seemingly innocuous look I know is actually full of snark and unsaid teases. "Been a while since you've played beer pong. Do you think Trinity's shoulder has recovered?"

"Ha ha," I say dryly, shooting Molly a look. "She was fine."

Bryson looks between us. "Something happen?"

"Yes," Molly says, at the same time as I proclaim, "No."

Quinn crosses his arms over his chest and grins widely. "There's a story here."

"There's no story," I insist. "I'm just - I can be a little competitive, and it backfired once."

"A little competitive," Molly repeats, doubling over with laughter. "Okay, sure."

I rub the bridge of my nose, exasperated. "Look, it's fine. I've evolved since then. Let's play."

I'm lying. I've not evolved since the time two years ago when I launched myself at an innocent bystander Trinity in celebration of winning a point over Molly, accidentally causing Trinity to strain her shoulder. I've probably actually regressed, if anything; now that the only person I compete with is myself, I can be as tough as I want without the pesky addition of acknowledging how the other person is feeling.

But hey, Bryson and Quinn don't need to know that.

So, I tighten my ponytail, hoping that the sun isn't illuminating too much of the grey streak at the front that I've given up on hiding, and beat Molly in rock-paper-scissors.

On the upside, it turns out that Bryson is also a bit of a liar. He's not terrible at beer pong at all. About ten tosses in, he and I have three cups left to Molly and Quinn's four. Both of the points we have against the other team were scored by Bryson.

It's my turn to throw next. I line myself up a perfect shot with the closest cup, take a deep breath, and toss the ball. It hits the rim, slides along the edge, and then funnels itself into the cup, landing with a silent splash in the half-filled beer.

"Yeah!" I exclaim, followed quickly by a loud whoop from Bryson. I pump my fists in the air in celebration and turn to him, expecting a high-five.

Instead, I find myself hoisted in the air, Bryson's strong arms around my waist and let out a quick yelp and grab at his shoulders. "Yeah, Carleigh!" he's saying excitedly, likely not even realizing that he's swinging me a bit to the side until my left foot finds the ground and I nearly stumble. Immediately, he steadies me with a big hand on my hip, one of his fingers brushing against the soft skin of my stomach where my tank top has ridden up slightly in the excitement. "Oops, I got you!"

I laugh and look up at him, suddenly glad I'm wearing sunglasses because god knows what sort of dumb look is on my face right now. "Thanks, Bryson."

"No casualties on my watch, babe, don't worry," he proclaims. Then, with a flip of his middle finger across the table, he grins. "Eat our dust, Quinn!"

"We're only tied now, Bryson," Quinn fires back. "Don't count your chickens!"

"Your chickens," Molly cuts in, giggling. "My god-

I hand Bryson the ball, reluctantly stepping out from his grasp to allow him to line up his shot. The ball flies past the end of the table. "Ooh, damn."

"I'll get you next time, Quinn!" Bryson promises. "Sorry, Carleigh."

"Oh, it's okay." A lie. It's not okay. Molly and Quinn must be destroyed.

As Molly preps for her turn, Bryson slings a casual arm over my shoulder and leans against me gently. Curiously, I find myself suddenly a bit more willing to forgive him for his bad shot.

We end up losing after quite a prolonged one-cup-remaining standoff. I'm proud of the fight we put up against Molly, who I know to be a very worthy beer pong competitor. It makes the sting of the loss a little easier to bear. The other thing easing the loss is Bryson, whose upbeat attitude is a little infectious. Besides, with each additional beer, he seems to be getting a little looser with his casual touching, too, and I'm not mad at it. But that's beside the point. Clearly.

After beer pong, I play a game of ladder golf against a friendly guy named Bishop. At this point, the sun is high in the sky and it's hot enough outside that a cold beer sounds pretty good, so I let Molly cajole me into having a couple of light beers. I'm a self-admitted lightweight, but it's not enough to make me feel uninhibited, though my insides do feel warm and more relaxed than usual.

At some point, somebody sets up a kiddie pool with a few inches of cold water from the hose. My legs are pretty tired from that morning's training run, and my feet are even more so, especially after standing around outside all day, so after the game with Bishop I go over to join Sawyer and

Royce in sticking my feet in the water. The grass surrounding it is a little wet, which I'm sure is probably creating a really attractive damp spot on the back of my jean shorts, but it's hot enough outside that I'm also sure it'll dry immediately.

The cold water is a shock to my system at first, but that feeling is quickly overtaken by a wave of relief. I sigh, happily. "Oh, that's great."

Royce smiles at me. "Remarkable how much just cooling your feet down helps out, isn't it?"

"Definitely," Sawyer agrees. "Royce, I know I've said it a hundred times, but I just love that blue polish color. It's perfect."

My eyes fall to Royce's fingernails, which are painted the same deep blue color as his toes. It is a gorgeous blue. "Really nice," I agree, suddenly feeling self-conscious about my bare toenails - about my feet generally, which I've kept callused and rough from running. "I should've thrown on some cheap red polish or something for Independence Day," I add thoughtfully. "Next year."

"I've got some blue polish in my bag," Royce offers. "I mean, mine is shellac, but I keep a spare regular polish in a close enough color on hand. Just to patch any chips until I can get them redone, you know."

"Oh, I wouldn't want to impose."

"No problem," he cuts in, dragging his feet out of the pool. He hops up and disappears into the house.

I slip my feet out as well and inspect them a little closer. I grimace at Sawyer. "I should've gotten a pedicure, probably."

Sawyer shrugs and smiles at me reassuringly. "It's all good. Royce'll fix you up. His specialty."

"Yeah?"

She nods. "He's been dedicated to that same polish for a few years now, knows his way around nails."

I run my hand along the heel of my foot. "I'm training for a marathon right now and my feet are kind of vile from that," I explain. "The calluses are good to keep for that."

"Oh really?" Sawyer asks, clearly interested. "I was thinking about doing something like that next spring. When is it?"

"Middle of August. So, it's ramping up right away. Today was a pretty light run, but my legs are still tired, somehow." I give a soft laugh. "I might not make it to August at this rate."

Royce returns then, holding a bottle of navy polish, a small bag, and an old towel, which he hands to me. "Dry your feet," he instructs, opening up the small bag to reveal a small manicurist's set.

I do so obediently. Royce sits down, pulls one of my feet into his lap, and begins pushing back the cuticles. There's no way he hadn't very clearly noticed the rough edges of my foot, and I feel compelled to explain that the calluses are intentional.

"Oh good," he says, relieved. "I was hoping you weren't a barefoot lunatic like Bryson."

I laugh. I'm aware of Bryson's dislike of shoes, even if I didn't actually see it that often in the city. It's just impractical. "No, I wear shoes," I promise. "Anyway, Sawyer, if you really are interested, I'd be happy to share my training plan with you."

"Yeah, that would be great," Sawyer says, nodding fervently. "I mean, I still might be too lazy, but it's good to have all the information before I sign up for something on a whim."

"Absolutely." I slip my phone out of my back pocket, find the plan I'd paid for in the carefully labeled 'fitness' section of my inbox, and set the email to forward. Then hand it to Sawyer. "Just toss your email in there and it should be good to go."

"Ooh Carleigh, giving out numbers?" a loud voice interrupts.

I glance up, squinting at the glare from the sun. The giant shadow moves, blocking the sun from my eyes, and I realize it's Bryson.

10

CARLEIGH

"What?" I ask.

He sits down beside me and drops his already bare feet into the kiddie pool. "Giving out numbers," he repeats. "To Sawyer! Careful Sawyer, Carleigh's a high-maintenance date. She'll make you watch a lot of Bravo."

I roll my eyes and carefully withdraw my foot from Royce at his direction. One sparkly coat of blue is on, and it looks great already. "Nobody's making you watch *Below Deck*, Bryson. Just admit you secretly love it."

"Absolutely not." He leans over until his chin is nearly over my shoulder and peers at Royce. "What's going on here, spa day? You doing me next?"

Royce looks up and gives him a withering look. "I don't know where those feet have been. Never."

"Your loss," Bryson answers cheerfully, and wiggles his feet in the water. "These feet would be so pretty, all twinkle-toes!"

"Hmm." I look at Sawyer across the kiddie pool and barely manage to suppress a laugh.

Bryson scoops a little water with his hand and sprays it playfully in my direction. "What'd I tell you about slandering Jersey, Carleigh?"

"I'm not slandering New Jersey!" I protest, raising a hand to protect myself. "I'm slandering your feet!"

"My feet are New Jersey, Carleigh."

"That doesn't even make sense, Bryson - eek!" I squeal, as he sprays an even larger bit of water at me.

"Bryson," Royce cuts in sharply, clutching my foot tighter to immobilize it. "Do not interrupt my work. You can wait ten more minutes to flirt, can't you?"

I press my lips together, fighting a smile despite the flush that reaches my cheeks. I manage a side glance at Bryson, and am surprised to see he doesn't look embarrassed at all.

"Yeah, I can wait ten minutes." Bryson taps the back of my hand with his wet fingers. "Come find me when the spa's closed, Murphy," he tells me, then hops to his feet and is gone.

I worry for a moment that Royce or Sawyer is going to press me about the whole lot of nothing that's going on between me and Bryson, but Royce snaps his fingers and announces, "Alright girl, second coat."

I intend to look for Bryson after my toes are painted, I really do, but Molly finds me first. She's holding two plastic cups and is wearing a big grin. "Carleigh!" she says excitedly. "Margarita time! And soon hot dogs!"

"Margarita, huh?" I sniff the drink, then take a small sip. "Oh, Molly, this tastes really good."

"Jackson mixed it," Molly says. "He has a crazy alcohol

selection." She sways a little on the spot to the song that's playing from the Bluetooth speaker that's set up by the fire pit, then waggles her eyebrows at me. "So, you and ol' blue eyes, hmmm?"

I scoff and shake my head, but I get where Molly's coming from. Based on today - and okay, on the past couple of weeks, where it seems like just maybe Bryson didn't always need to touch me as much as he had - it does seem like things might be shifting-- slightly. But that's just to the untrained eye - Molly doesn't know Bryson that well. He's just an affectionate guy who cares about his friends. Right?

A sudden wave of anxiety-induced nausea overtakes me, and I swallow hard. What a lunatic; of course, it's all in my head. What am I even doing?

Molly sips her drink and gives an exaggerated shrug. "Oh, Carleigh," she says. "He's definitely into you, I promise."

"Shh," I hiss. The last thing I need is for any of Bryson's friends to overhear; how pathetic would that be?

"Fine, I'll drop it," Molly acquiesces. "But down the hatch with that drink, girl. Get out of your own head."

I obediently take another sip. I'm willing to indulge a little more than usual today, but still pacing myself; I don't think my liver will suddenly understand the concept of living in the moment.

"Good girl," Molly praises. She tilts my shoulders toward the beer pong table, where I spot Bryson once again providing a faux-sports announcer's commentary on a game. "I need to use the bathroom. Now go be social!"

I flash a half-hearted warning look at Molly, but hey, Bryson did tell me to come find him. So I approach, my newly-painted feet brushing against the soft grass, and stand a couple of feet away from him near the table.

"Who's winning?" I ask, more as a means to announce my presence. It's clear that Quinn is absolutely destroying Bishop.

Bryson turns around. "Carleigh!" he exclaims, clearly a bit intoxicated. He reaches out with one long arm and beckons me to come closer. "Come here, get right on the fifty-yard line," he instructs, tugging me just in front of him to the middle of the board. He sets a hand on my shoulder. "Quinn is wiping the floor with Bhati. Just a complete annihilation."

"It's not over yet, Bryson," Bishop says, a hint of annoyance in his voice. "You have to believe."

"Right. Sorry, sorry," Bryson apologizes. "You got this, bud!" He lifts his hand from my shoulder and holds it up in exaggerated surrender, then drops it to my waist and squeezes gently. "Right?"

I nod and smile at Bishop. "A comeback is definitely on the horizon," I assure him.

"As if," Quinn scoffs, lining up a shot. "I'm about to end this man."

"He shoots -" Bryson says in a loud tone, halting to watch Quinn throw the ball. "-oh! And he misses! This is it, Bhati, this is your moment!"

I watch Bishop walk a few feet behind the table to retrieve the ball from the grass. "Maybe it really is a comeback," I muse.

As my eyes follow Bishop, two fingers tap my hip. I glance up and see Bryson smiling down at me. "Hey," he says, his voice suddenly quiet. His curls are beginning to escape from beneath his ball cap. "Your toes look nice."

"Thanks," I say, the corners of my lips turning up. *Come on Carleigh, live in the moment.* I turn my gaze back to the table and shift my weight backward, just a little, testing the waters.

He doesn't move at first, and I'm immediately convinced that either I've misread the entire situation, or I've been too subtle - which is a possibility with Bryson, for whom subtlety doesn't seem to be popular. But then one beat later, Bryson's hand shifts on my hip: his thumb slips through the empty belt loop of my shorts and the rest of his fingers curl to rest against the denim. His feet don't move, but he seems to have swayed forward - that, or I'm so aware of his presence that it feels like his chest is almost flush against my back. I'm reminded for the millionth time that he's ridiculously tall.

Bishop scores against Quinn. This time, Bryson doesn't fist-pump. Instead, he raises his left arm and beer bottle upward and lets out a "Whoop!" keeping his other arm where it is. I assume it's part of some kind of exaggerated toast, but I like to think that just maybe it's because he doesn't want to let go.

"Come on, one of you hurry up and lose," Royce calls, from his perch by the kiddie pool. "I was promised hot dogs like twenty-minutes ago."

The rest of the afternoon passes almost in a blur, but I have clear memories of a few moments. Eating dinner on the grass. Bryson winking at me across the rough circle. Molly's elbow happily nudging my ribs from beside me. Teaming up with Molly to beat Max and Royce at beer pong, this time downing the vile warm beer in the bottom of the cups,

Bryson laughing at the face I make from where he's watching nearby.

When dusk begins to settle, Quinn whistles to get everyone's attention. He announces it's time to start walking to where they'll watch the fireworks.

"Don't forget, we're coming right back afterward - all those bars around there are a rip-off tonight."

Fine with me. I'm happy to do a little walking and stretch my legs out; for the last twenty-minutes, I've been curled up with Molly and a diluted margarita on the grass, and my calves are starting to cramp up. Some movement and a break from drinking will be good for everyone, probably.

Everyone files out of the backyard, leaving their empties and half-empties behind for Bishop and another guy, whose name I don't remember, to monitor - not fireworks fans, apparently - and settle in a few chaotic columns down the sidewalk.

I fall in alongside Sawyer and Molly. We spend most of the twenty-minute walk talking about cycling, since apparently Sawyer's interest in running also extends a little to triathlons, and Molly had been a cycling buddy of Trinity's. None of them seem to like lane swimming, which I point out is probably at least a little bit because of the expense of membership at a facility with a decently-sized pool in Manhattan.

Jersey City's fireworks are over the Hudson this year, which should look pretty great with the Manhattan skyline just behind. Bryson's friends' viewing spot is apparently a park with views across the river. Upon arrival, it's also several thousand other people's optimal viewing spot.

"That's because Morris Canal's got grass," Quinn pipes

in, when Molly comments on how busy it is. "People watch from Exchange Place, too, and some bars, but it's all boardwalk and wood there."

As a short person, I'm always a little worried about seeing, but I'm comforted by the fact that at least this is fireworks - high in the sky above everybody, even tall people like Bryson. Still, as we enter the crowd in an attempt to carve out a spot on the grass, I'm feeling the downsides of being small. I get separated from Molly and Sawyer by a family with two double strollers and have to scurry between people to catch up. In the process, someone steps on my foot, but my yelp is lost in the crowd. I lean down to make sure everything is fine - can't take any chances with the marathon coming up - and when I stand up, I realize I'm lost again.

Just as I can feel my frustration start to boil over, Bryson is magically at my side.

"Knew you'd get lost in a crowd, Murphy," he says jokingly. "Should have given you one of the beacons they give to people at sea."

"Ha ha," I say dryly, but I'm ecstatic to see him. He offers one of his hands, and I take it gratefully.

"Don't let go," Bryson instructs, then proceeds to cut a beeline through the crowd. I stick close behind, hurrying two steps for his one, letting his large frame make an easy path to follow, until finally the crowd breaks, and I see our group getting settled on a free swath of grass a little ways away from the main horde.

"You found her!" Royce exclaims from where he's sitting, Molly to his right, Sawyer beside her.

"I got cut off by a stroller," I explain, slightly out of breath.

"Thought we had to send the police in," Quinn teases.

I roll my eyes. "I'm an excellent navigator. I would've found my way eventually. Just look for Bryson!"

"I'm hard to miss, babe," he agrees cheerfully. "Now come on, sit down before these firecrackers start!"

I look over my shoulder briefly to find an empty spot, but it's still a little crowded here, too, and I'm met with a couple of glares from families already seated behind them. There's a momentary sense of panic, until Bryson folds himself down where he stands and tugs me down, too, by the hand he's still holding.

"The ground isn't made for tall people either," he grumbles, looking uncomfortable with his knees half-up to his shoulders.

I give him a sympathetic look. "At least you always have a great view?"

Bryson laughs. "I've got an idea – come here." He turns to the side and slides his legs forward, then parts his knees, and pats the ground in front of him. "Free backrest," he offers.

A breeze rolls through, but I've had enough to drink that it doesn't chill me. Even so, I'm not going to say no to his body heat. So, I nod and turn, shuffling in reverse on my ass until his arms reach forward, wrap around my waist, and haul me fully backward.

"This okay?" Bryson asks, his voice cheerful in my ear.

My legs look tiny between his. "Yeah," I say, turning my head halfway before swiveling back and picking a few blades of grass off my knees.

I'm not sure I'm going to be able to withstand just how overwhelming it feels to have his body surrounding mine, his knees on either side, his arms around my waist, his hands settled in my lap. I rest my forearms on top of his and lean into him, letting my weight falls against his chest. He smells like the outdoors; like grass, sweat, and beer, like Bryson. It's a lot.

I'm so glad Molly is in front of us, because I don't think I'll ever hear the end of it if my friend turns around and sees us basically cuddling here in this park.

Then, the faint music that's been playing all around gets a little louder, and the fireworks show starts. Fireworks are overrated, honestly - something explodes, it looks cool for a while, people clap, and then you're all just alone in the dark with the mosquitoes - but tonight, they seem beautiful. Tonight, the colors seem extra bright, the designs impressive, and Manhattan behind them looks like the best place on earth.

"Still wishing you were at the apartment watching Bravo?" Bryson says into my ear.

I turn my head to the side, my cheek against his shoulder, and shake my head. "No," I mumble, smiling into his sleeve. "No, I'm glad I'm here."

"I'm glad you're here, too." He grips the outside of my thigh, just behind my knee, and squeezes affectionately.

It's then I realize just truly how messed up I am: because all I want right now is for that big hand to move higher up my thigh, for his fingers to slide between my legs, his big mouth hot on my neck. I want to turn around and drag him away behind the trees and find out just how strong he really is. And then - then, I want him to hold me after, just like he is now, sweet and caring and genuine.

I'm wholly, truly, and desperately attracted to my roommate.

11

BRYSON

On a Monday approximately one week after the Independence Day weekend, two things of opposing merit happen to me. Chronologically speaking, the event that happens first is the shitty one.

It's mid-morning and I'm at a site near the docks in Red Hook, of all places. We're fixing the concrete barriers around a crumbling strip of access road – not the most inspired project, but the docks are pretty interesting to watch from a bit of a distance. Since it's mid-July, the heat is starting to rise from the pavement; I can already feel the sweat accruing in the middle of my back and am grateful my work shirt is dark in color, or else I'd have to wear my safety vest on the train home to hide the stains on my shirt.

The stupid thing: I'm paying attention when the accident happens. I may be doing a little musing – there's a good fish market nearby I've been to before, and I figure if I'm done early enough today to snag something half-decent on the way home, I can make fish tacos for dinner – but it's no more daydreaming than usual. I'm focused on hauling away the stray smaller blocks of crumbling concrete that our larger equipment left behind, using my big hands and a reinforced wheelbarrow to grab and clear off the sheared pieces – and then it happens.

There isn't supposed to be anything in this path, but someone has obviously neglected to clear away all the old rebar, because my work boot snags on a forgotten piece of the metal and I go crashing to the ground. My grip on the wheelbarrow doesn't release in time, it follows me to the pavement, and a hundred pounds of broken concrete pieces slam into my bicep. It's really terrible, because I'm actually pretty intense about safety on the work site, and I've never been injured before.

I get sent to the hospital in a cab.

Really, it's kind of an overreaction. My arm is bruised, and I get a few stitches near my elbow, but the scans are clear up there. Which is nothing: I've broken many bones in my life, including one time shattering my wrist trying to jump off Quinn's roof on a dare, and I know I could go back to work right away if it were just my arm.

My toes and feet are fine, thanks to steel-toed boots – this is why everyone is so up in arms about PPE, I want to shout – but the real problem is according to the doctor, I have a hairline fracture on my ankle. So, work is out for at least a few weeks, depending on how I feel and how healing is going. I have to fill out about a thousand reports for worker's compensation, all of which are infuriatingly annoying, then I get a big plastic boot to immobilize my leg, some painkillers, a pair of too-short crutches, and a cab home.

The hospital takes forever, so by the time I get dropped

off in front of my building, it's well past lunchtime. I decide I'm not willing to cook anything, so I haul my big plastic boot and my shitty crutches halfway up the block to the corner deli. I get a half of a giant lumberjack sandwich, shove it into the ankle of the work boot I'm also lugging around, then struggle my way back home and up to the apartment.

Then, the second thing happens. This one is, objectively speaking, better.

Once I step in front of the door, I can hear music playing and immediately recognize, "*Dancing in the Dark.*" Carleigh must be working on school stuff at home today instead of the library, though usually when she's working she demands absolute silence, so I'm a little surprised to hear the music. But hey, whatever works for her. I put my keys in the door and hobble inside.

I'm not delicate about it at all – not that I usually am, even without crutches and a boot – but the music is pretty loud, so Carleigh doesn't hear me right away. Which suits me fine, because when I walk in, my roommate is in our small kitchen in front of a squared-off sheet of pastry dough, wearing a fitted white sundress with little blue flowers printed on it, wet hair tied up in a knot on her head, barefoot. And she's dancing.

At the moment, I can't decide whether to be focused on how completely adorable it is or on how beautiful she looks. I did manage to convince her to come to New Jersey for July 4th and she seemed to have a good time, despite my total inability to keep my hands off of her, which I vow to try to control; just because she's polite about it doesn't mean it's welcomed.

Carleigh's been so stressed lately, with this marathon she's decided to run, and with what I gather are issues with her grad program, and I'm really happy to see her dancing around with a little smile on her face.

It doesn't last long. Carleigh turns slightly in my direction just as I'm setting my work boot-and-sandwich combo on the ground and shrieks when she notices she's not alone.

"Bryson, god, make a little noise," she breathes, one hand flying to her chest. Carleigh pulls her phone toward her, taps a couple of keys, and the music turns off.

"No one's ever had to tell me that before," I joke, flashing my best grin. "Sorry to interrupt, Murphy, it looked like a good party."

"Ha ha." Carleigh folds her arms. "I was just celebrating a little, I – oh my god, what happened?"

I hobble a little more clearly into her view and look around for a stool. I want to get this other work boot off already. "It's nothing, Carleigh, don't worry."

She's at my side a second later with one of the kitchen chairs. I sink into it and lean over to untie my shoe, but Carleigh swats at my hand and crouches in front of me. "I got it."

"Carleigh, no," I wince, very aware of the fact that my feet are going to smell. My first order of business probably actually should be having a shower – thankfully, this plastic boot comes off, and as long as I'm good to my ankle, I should be able to do all of that normally – and the last thing that I want is for Carleigh to get a full whiff of the mid-July construction scent.

She's more stubborn than I count on, though, and she begins to unlace my shoe anyway. To her credit, if it does stink, she doesn't let on – though when she sets the work boot aside, she does make a face at the sandwich that's sticking out of the matching one. "Is this your lunch?" she asks, picking it up by two fingers like it's made of fire.

I shrug. "Bought it on the corner. Mine got left at work when I got sent to the hospital, and I figured I was too lazy to whip up anything good here."

Carleigh shakes her head, then stands up and sets it on the counter. "So, what happened?"

"Tripped over some rebar," I answer. "Fell down and bunch of concrete came down with me. A couple of stitches on my arm, and it's sore, it's fine. My ankle's got a hairline fracture, though, so I'm off work 'til that heals."

"Oh no!" Carleigh bites her lip. "With worker's comp, I hope?"

I nod. "Yeah, should be. I had to fill out about a million forms."

I stand up, waving her away when she moves to help me. "I can walk, Carleigh, I'm just supposed to keep off it for the most part."

"Then let me help you! Lean on my shoulder."

I chuckle. "I got crutches for that. I'd probably crush you if you tried to hold me up."

Carleigh frowns. "Hey, I'm stronger than I look!"

"That's cute. You asked me to open a jar of peppercinis literally yesterday." I wink; she sticks her tongue out. "I have to take a shower. I was vile before I took a bath in the concrete, so I can't imagine how much worse it's gotten. But don't throw out my sandwich, I'm going to eat that."

"Oh, no you aren't. I'll make you something better."

Carleigh watches me as I take careful steps down the hallway. "Do you need help?" she asks, tone uncertain.

I turn around and grin. "Like, nurse Murphy gives me a sponge bath?"

Her cheeks flush pink. "No, like – do you need to wrap the ... this thing," she says, taking a couple of steps toward me and pointing at the boot.

"No, it comes off, I just have to be careful." Then, because I just can't help myself, I add, "So, you're saying the sponge bath is off the table?"

The blush from Carleigh's cheeks has spread to her chest now. It's so sweet, I can barely stand it. "We'll have to see how bad you get," she answers in a cool tone, eyes sparkling. "Now go, shower."

"Okay, okay," I agree, and hobble away.

After my shower, I changed into a pair of old shorts and a t-shirt, figuring that the lack of both sleeves and pant legs would allow me to better monitor the injuries. Plus, it's hot outside, and even though we have air conditioning, the apartment is pretty warm. Carleigh must be baking something.

I shuffle down to the living room and see Carleigh has set me up on the couch with the strategically-placed remote, an ice cold bottle of a local kombucha, and what looks like a vastly-improved version of my corner deli sandwich. I just settled down onto the good spot when she comes around the corner, holding a jar of my best half-sour pickles and looking vaguely apologetic.

"Sorry," Carleigh says by way of beginning. "I wanted to have it ready, but I need you to open this."

I smile at her, take the jar, and open it easily. When she gives me a wry look, I say, "You must've loosened it, babe."

Carleigh makes a face, but doesn't say anything as she drops a few pickles on my plate. I try to avoid it, but it's difficult not to notice the view down the top of her dress that she is providing me by leaning over my plate. I don't see anything untoward, mostly because the bodice is actually pretty slim-fitting compared to a lot of her clothes, but I'm now pretty aware she can't be wearing a bra with this dress.

She returns the jar to the kitchen and then comes back, sitting a polite distance away on the couch. "Does it hurt right now?" she asks, her brow wrinkled in concern.

"Not really, Carleigh, just kind of a dull ache." I jut my thumb in the direction of my bedroom. "I got some pain stuff. Nothing real fancy. Just extra-strength normal stuff." I click the TV on, then have a flash of memory from when I first arrived home. "Hey, what were you celebrating?"

"Huh?"

"When I got home," I clarify. "And you were having your one-woman dance party. You were saying you were celebrating something, then I horned in with my ankle and interrupted."

"Oh." Carleigh smiles and a light appears in her face. "I submitted a draft of this one tricky section of my paper to my supervising professor. Nothing really to celebrate, I guess, I've just been kind of struggling with it for the last few weeks I still have other sections and I'll definitely have more to do on this one later, too, once I get feedback, but it feels really good to have at least one kick at part of the can out the door."

"That's great!" I gesture to her phone. "Is that what Bruce was all about?"

Carleigh laughs. "Yeah. I've decided to take every small victory I can."

I clap my hands together. "That's the spirit! So, how are we celebrating?"

"Oh, it's not – it's not a real milestone," Carleigh dismisses. "It's not a real thing to celebrate. I was just letting off some steam."

I shrug and pick up my sandwich. "Who cares if it isn't real? Let's let off some steam. I'm a bit tougher to drag around right now, but let's do something fun. At least, turn Bruce back on!"

"I've got dough resting," Carleigh informs. "When it's ready for the oven, sure. I was also going to go to the store to get stuff for dinner…"

"We can order in." I point to my leg. "I'm hurt, remember? Sick person gets to pick."

Carleigh rolls her eyes. "That's not a real thing, but okay, twist my arm. Don't pick something vile, though." She tucks her legs up beside her delicately, sticking her toes between the cushions, and leans in my direction. There's still about two feet between us, which is a normal distance to leave between friends, but right now I'm feeling a little cuddlier than usual.

So, I lift an arm up and gestures for her to move closer. "Come here. I don't stink anymore."

There's no hesitation on her part, which I know has to be because we've built up a pretty good level of base physical affection at this point, so it's not weird anymore. I'm a hugger, always have been, and she constantly seems like she needs one. Simple as that.

Plus, Quinn isn't here to give me the side-eye like he did all of July 4th. I don't have to justify myself to anyone except Carleigh, and she seems perfectly content to sit here against my chest with my arm around her waist and watch reruns of *Top Gear*. The only problem now is I have to finish eating this sandwich one-handed.

I manage to do so without dropping anything, then offer one of the pickles to Carleigh. She turns and smiles her thanks, then takes it.

"Ooh this is good, Bryson."

"Thanks." I follow suit and have to agree; one of my better batches, for sure. "Half-sour, just like you," I joke, which earns me a swat to my leg. I slide my plate on the coffee table and prop the foot up beside it. "Thanks for the late lunch, too. Definitely better than the deli."

"Of course, it was." Carleigh leans even further into me. She stretches both feet out at a slight angle to mine, settling them on the coffee table as well. Then, to my amusement, she reaches behind herself, grabs my arm, and pulls it around her.

I can't help but laugh softly. "Yeah, just get comfy, Half-Sour."

"Yeah, I will." The teasing lilt is evident in her voice as Carleigh points at the TV. "What is this show, anyway? What's with the cars?"

"I don't know, it was the first recommendation. Just trying to find something that isn't Bravo-based." I play my fingers against her ribcage, tickling lightly.

Carleigh scoffs. "You are just as into *Real Housewives* as I am now, don't even lie."

"I will never admit that." I flip the TV to Planet Earth. "This better?" I ask. "Warning you, this might put me to sleep for an hour."

"Oh, Bryson, if you're tired, I can leave you alone," Carleigh says immediately, moving to sit up. "I'll mess up your sleep."

I tighten my grip. "Don't go nowhere," I say, even as I close my eyes. "You stand guard while ol' Bryson naps."

"I'll do my best," she reports, and I remember nothing after.

I wake up slowly.

I know I haven't been asleep for that long – an hour at best – because my post-work naps, if I take them, are never that intense. Plus, Planet Earth is still playing, and I've still got Carleigh under my arm. Her feet are back curled beneath herself and she's deep in my side and breathing even now; her eyes are closed.

My thumb moves against her dress, stroking lightly. She sighs, shifts a little, but doesn't wake.

Damn it. I just had to go get Carleigh as a roommate. I couldn't have found some grease ball on Craigslist. Just had to listen to Morocco, and I had to find this funny, smart, beautiful woman. And now I'm in too deep – now I'm laughing with her, cuddling with her, now I never want to go out again, so that I have a reason to sit here on this couch and hold her.

Because I'm a big sap and she's here, so pretty and comfy and small against me, I got my other arm, stitches and bruises and all, involved in this mess. I'm lifting it and bringing it over and my fingers are sliding her hair away from where it's caught against her neck, all so I don't have to move my other hand from where it rests on her waist. It gives me a beautiful line of sight across her neck, over her collarbones, to where her pale skin swells and then disappears under the dress, and then beyond. I gently wrap my hand around her slim bicep, thumb on the outside.

Her skin is cold to the touch and I suspect that either the A/C has kicked in or the heat from the oven has faded, so I lean my head against the back of the couch, close my eyes, and rub her arm slowly, nearly absentmindedly, only faintly aware of the soft press of her right breast against the back of my knuckles.

When Carleigh stirs some unknown amount of time later, I still my hand.

"Sorry," I apologize, whispering as quietly as I can, like if I barely say it and she barely hears it, it means it barely happened.

But she does. "It's okay," she breathes, reaching one of her hands up to settle over mine. "You don't have to apologize. It feels nice."

"Oh," I say back, feeling dumb.

Carleigh gently unwinds herself from my hands. She looks a little pink when she sits up. "I better go check on my dough," she says, in what almost seems like a regretful tone. "How's your ankle?"

"Hurts," I admit. "I should probably take another painkiller." I lift my foot off the table and wince when it finds the floor.

"I can get them," Carleigh offers, but I decline.

"I have to pee, too, but thanks anyway." I make an exaggerated show of groaning as I stand, but my bones do hurt a little; god, I really need to find a better line of work than one that's going to crush my body by the time I'm forty.

Carleigh is still peering at me with concern. "You sure you're okay, Bryson?" she asks, her fingertips delicately touching my injured bicep.

"Right as rain." I open my arms for a hug, hoping it's not too forward, like I didn't just spend the last hour and some with her in my arms already. "Thanks for taking care of me."

Carleigh steps in and lets me fold my arms around her. "I didn't do anything," she says, voice muffled against my chest.

Clearly, I've given up my vow from earlier to not touch her as much. I'll start again after my leg is better. Right now, I just want a hug, and she fits so well and smells so good and she's so soft, and it's honestly impossible not to want to run my palms across her bare upper back when she's wearing this dress. Which I do, only half-ashamedly, but she makes a happy-sounding noise into my shirt and hugs me back just as tightly.

"Well, there's always that sponge bath," I say, cutting the tension with a joke when I finally manage to pull back from her.

Carleigh's eyes dance as she laughs. "Play your cards right with your takeout choice and we'll see," she teases, then disappears into the kitchen.

I'm a goner.

12

CARLEIGH

I'm standing in a beautifully decorated reception area, wearing a fancier dress than I care to, clutching a glass of white wine so tightly in my hand that I think it might shatter. If it happens, and hits the beautiful floor of this hall, it'll be the university's fault. Actually, all of this is Columbia University's fault.

It's a reception hosted by my grad program, a sort of mini-gala dinner in honor of a visiting professor, held at my university's best venue - Faculty House, home of many a bat mitzvah and wedding - which inexplicably had been scheduled for mid-summer, when many of my fellow lit grads are not around to attend. Of course, I'm around – I always am, always in the student carrels of the library or in search of coffee somewhere in these hallowed buildings - so I get a free ticket for the dinner. Get two free tickets, actually, and am asked - ordered - to bring someone, so as to fill up space.

That, of course, is the last thing I want to do. Obviously, I love lectures. I'm a nerd in the truest sense; love podcasts, love learning, love listening to old guys drone on and on about history and literature and everything else. And I attend a grad program with a bunch of other people who also love all of those things. The problem is those are the only people I know who would be at all interested in attending, and they're all already invited.

Of them, only my friend and fellow grad student Evana is actually coming. She's bringing her boyfriend, but he's doing his Ph.D. in classics, so he's used to these sorts of things. They're a great couple, really fun people, so at a minimum I know I'll have a great time third-wheeling.

But then: enter Bryson.

I've been on the phone with Molly, trying in vain to convince her to ditch her family's annual vacation to California so she could attend a lecture for a literature graduate program - it's a clear failure from the beginning, but I owe it to my professors to actually try - when Bryson walked into the living room, pieced my dilemma together, and offered to come.

I'll admit, I've been a little bit nervous about it. First, there is the whole thing where I'm extremely into him and trying desperately not to make it obvious so as to save myself the embarrassment of rejection - plus, we live together, what a terrible idea from many angles - but besides that, the concern is about the general hoity-toity attitude of my cohort. Evana is cool, I'm not worried about Evana - but the professors, the school, the whole shebang - it all screams classism. I've got some merit funding, but the bottom line is I'm still spending thousands of dollars to live in Manhattan to attend Columbia University to get a master's degree in literature, and after this I'll probably end up spending even more money to get a Ph.D. and then spend the rest of my life in academic institutions. If Bryson doesn't already think I'm stuffy and out of touch, he probably will after this.

Secretly, I'd love to go to pastry school and work in a bakery; I hate the idea of the early hours, but I would love the work. That, though, doesn't fit into my five-year plan.

Not that I don't love being in school - I really, really do. It's the thing I've always been best at. I'm not friendly or outgoing or naturally charming enough to be instantly liked. I'm an introvert, bossy, and particular. All of the things that have made me into a neurotic person with only a few good friends also make me an excellent student – and probably a decent teacher - so really, academic life is probably what I'm best suited for. I can live locked up in my ivory tower with all the other people who are just like me.

Bryson is decidedly not one of those people. He's the opposite of me in so many respects - he's funny, warm, and charismatic. He's spontaneous, distracted, and full of life in the kind of way that the stuffy professorial types at my school would deride. He's got a gift, a way with other people, that even with all of the training in the world, I could never learn. And whether or not he realizes it, it'll take him anywhere he wants to go.

I'm pretty sure Bryson could turn the dictator of North Korea into being a friend. Who I have less faith in are the more conservative, uptight people in my cohort.

Of course, in the end, I'm wrong. Everybody loves him. His warm grin and easy nature are contagious, and if it wasn't for him muttering, "I'm so damn out of place here, Carleigh," into my ear when we walked in, I would've thought that it was a perfect fit from all sides.

It actually works too well. This is Columbia's fault. They didn't need to schedule this at a time where I have to bring my roommate that I have poorly suppressed feelings for. It didn't need to be semi-formal in the annoying way the Ivy types like everything to be. I don't need to be wearing this blue dress -though I do look pretty good in it: it's dusty blue, with short sleeves, and stretches from just beneath my collarbone to just above my knees. Professional enough for the setting, but it also gathers into a knot at the left side of my waist, so I'm not completely shapeless.

Bryson doesn't need to be dressed up either. I'm kind of embarrassed to note his being cleaned up a little is probably the most distracting thing about tonight. His hair is half-tamed, no hat, curls just wild enough to still be him. He's wearing a pair of dress pants with a black button-up shirt tucked in, and shoes that aren't slip-on or steel-toed work boots. It's alternate-universe semi-corporate Bryson, kind of, and while I'm sure he's not comfortable, he looks really, really good.

I'm not the only one who's noticed.

I really should've seen this coming. I came to a party for repressed overachievers and brought a tall, well-built, good-looking man. A man who'd never met a stranger and who immediately engaged anyone interested in conversation.

So, that is how I end up here, with a vice grip on the only glass of wine I've let myself have tonight, standing at a reception-height table with Evana and her boyfriend, Han, watching an English-lit grad student named Ashley, who once asked me if I dressed like a nun on purpose, flirt heavily with Bryson one table over.

"Ashley's friendly," I observe, keeping my tone of voice as measured and careful as possible.

"More like a wolf waiting to strike," Evana corrects, taking a large sip of bourbon. "And your roommate is a little baby deer who wandered into her territory."

I snort. I really love Evana.

"If the wolf actually just wants to get the baby deer," Ham adds. "More like a praying mantis."

Evana nods and taps her index finger against Han's thumb. "Yeah, that's a better analogy." She nudges me. "So, anything going on there?"

I take a small sip of wine. "We're just friends."

"You guys look good together."

I smile as my head shakes at Evana. I would never introduce her to Molly. "Bryson is 6'4," He looks good with everybody."

"You should probably go rescue him from Ashley." Evana raises an eyebrow in their direction.

I glance over, see Ashley laughing and touching Bryson's forearm. It looks strong and tanned against his rolled-up sleeve - I may not like Ashley, but I have to admit, she has good taste. He's a grown man and he can do whatever he wants.

Evana, apparently undeterred, calls over, "Hey, Bryson! Come here for a second."

I try to keep my face neutral, but I feel an overwhelming sense of pleasure at the way Ashley looks affronted when Bryson politely excuses himself. He stands next to me, holding a glass of red wine in one hand, and sets his other on my lower back. Ashley makes a face, walks away, and I'm on cloud nine.

"What's up?" he asks.

"Nothing," Evana says dismissively, knocking back the rest of her bourbon. "Just saving you. Ashley's a snake in the grass."

Bryson looks curiously at me, who shrugs and then nods. "Oh," he says. "Okay."

An announcement is made that the lecture and dinner portion is about to begin, so we grab our drinks and begin to file into the adjacent room, where round tables with cloth napkins and real silverware have been set up. Mercifully, Bryson and I are seated with Han and Evana, as well as a girl I recognize as being from the history department and her date, a guy who looks like he's already bored.

I'm just setting my wine down when Bryson reaches over from where he's seated beside me and taps my knee. "Here, switch seats with me. I'm going to be blocking your view."

"Trust me, Bryson, a better view isn't going to make or break this," I reply, but he looks at me insistently, so I agree, rising from the seat and then taking his. Once he's settled, I lean over and quietly ask, "How's your ankle?"

Bryson lifts up the edge of his pant leg to show me the tensor bandage that's wrapped securely around his injured ankle. He's been off work for a few weeks ever since he got hurt, but it seems to be doing very well, and at his last appointment the doctor gave him the go-ahead to take the boot off, so long as he isn't straining or overworking his ankle. "Doing just fine, babe, don't worry."

Waiters appear seemingly all at the same time, and begin placing starter salads at each place setting. This one appears to have slices of fresh peaches and crumbled feta across what looks like arugula; it looks pretty good.

"Great balsamic," Bryson comments, after taking a bite. "Really nice."

I smile. "You never met an acid you didn't like, huh?"

"What's not to like, Carleigh?" he says cheerfully.

The main course is a beautiful arrangement of roast beef and new potatoes, which I scarf down quickly; I skipped lunch in an effort to finish a set of revisions before this event tonight, and I'm starving, especially after the long training run this morning. After that, a small dish of lemon gelato is served over shortbread for dessert. It's a little dry, but before I can comment on it to Bryson - not that he cares, but I'll tell him anyway - the lecture begins.

It's actually fairly interesting; the speaker is a visiting professor from Montreal, who talks about fictional depictions of wartime restrictions on domestic life, and the effect of that representation on secondary-level history texts. It's forty minutes long, a merciful length considering all the non-lit people who are in attendance, and the speaker is both dynamic and clear enough to be accessible for the whole audience. I sneak a peek at Bryson throughout the lecture, hoping he's at least not falling asleep in his chair, but every time I see him he's rapt with attention, back straight, brow slightly furrowed, like he's trying to take it all in. The only evidence of his usual manic personality is his knee bouncing quietly.

When the professor finishes, everybody claps politely. Evana, who'd had to turn her chair completely to look at the lecturer, turns to the table and remarks, "Good length. I wonder if he's done any work as far as questioning the absence of regulatory schemes for some of these publishers."

"Is that even a thing?" Bryson asks. He looks at me. "Probably a stupid question, but isn't that kind of in opposition to freedom of speech?"

"Good point, Bryson," I say. He smiles. "I wonder that, too, Evana - but Bryson's right. You can publish whatever you want. It's everybody else that assigns it some kind of trustworthiness."

Evana nods slowly. "So maybe the better question then is around professional historical associations, and why they aren't doing more to speak out against inaccuracies. Wartime rationing maybe isn't the hill to die on, but..."

"People don't usually go into fields of study to police them, though," Han offers. "You have to have people who are willing to make a big deal out of it."

"Maybe no one's doing it for history and whatever, but I see people on TV all the time talking about science," Bryson says. "Scientists. Real smarty pants like you guys. Talking 'about climate change and vaccines and stuff."

I nod and tap my low-heeled sandal against Bryson's shoe under the table and smile at him when he looks over.

"So, that probably goes back to Evana's point... about this topic not being a hill to die on," Ham says. "But people are willing to do it when it matters?"

"At least with politicized and higher-profile things like climate change, there's certainly more of an incentive to." The room is starting to clear out; I fold my napkin and place it on the table. We've already spent enough time schmoozing with my professors and their colleagues. Really, I should probably do a little more networking, but I'm tired and despite his obvious engagement with the lecture, I don't want to drag this out any more for Bryson.

"You around here next week, Carleigh?" Evana asks, as she stands and picks up her bag from the back of the chair.

"Should be."

Evana flashes a thumbs up. "Cool, see you then. Bye Bryson, it was nice to meet you."

"Same to you," Bryson says to both her and her date, then they turn and make their way to the exit.

I push my chair in and step to Bryson's side. "Let's get out of here before I have to talk to anyone else about school," I mutter, eliciting a laugh from him.

"One ninja sneak-out, coming right up." He offers a hand, ostensibly to help me wind through the circular tables as we leave, but once we're back in the reception hall and headed toward the exit, he doesn't make a move to drop it, and I don't either.

13

CARLEIGH

It's dark once we step outside into the night air, but it's not that late yet - about ten. We turn and walk south. When we pass by the church, I grip his hand tighter and tug him across the street to Morningside Park.

"We can cut across the park," I suggest. "It'll be easier to get a cab on the other side."

"Sure." Bryson points at my shoes. "You okay to walk in those?"

"They're not that high," I say, "it's fine. I should ask you, actually - is your ankle okay? We can just call an Uber."

"I'm right as rain, babe, don't worry." He squeezes my hand. "Thanks for bringing me tonight. I was a little worried at the start there, but it actually was interesting."

I laugh. "Thank you for coming. I can't believe I got you out without a hat."

Bryson runs his free hand through his hair. "I clean up pretty good though, huh?" he says, with a grin. "I should have worn my bow tie."

I roll my eyes. "All that attention is going to your head already. Should've let Ashley hook her claws into you and take you to her lair."

"No." He waves his hand, swatting the implication away.

"Bryson, she was about to climb you like a tree before Evana called you away. No wonder you wear a hat all the time. The full effect is just too powerful."

He wiggles his eyebrows. "That so?" he teases, waving his hand at himself. "You feeling under the influence of fancy Bryson?"

I giggle and then scoff. Yes. But he doesn't need to know that. "I must have stronger willpower than Ashley."

Bryson clutches his chest. "You wound me, Carleigh!" he jokes. Then, distracted, he points our joined hands at a large tree we're passing by. "Hey, look at how big that squirrel's tail is!"

I follow his direction, spot the big rodent, and nod. Only Bryson would think to comment on that. "Very impressive," I confirm, using my free hand to rub my bare arm. It's still pretty warm, but it's getting a little cooler, and I'm sure the mosquitoes are about to come eat me alive any second. We're almost through the park, though, so it shouldn't be too much longer before...

Bryson stops walking, drops my hand, and all of a sudden, I'm warm again.

"You should have said you were cold," he says over the top of my head, his hands running across my back in big, wide strokes. "I should have noticed. You're wearing this little dress-"

I melt into his chest. God, I love hugging Bryson, love being held by him, and love how warm and affectionate he is. "It's summer," I mumble against his shirt. "The dress is for summer."

"Believe me, no complaints about the dress." A big palm runs down my bicep and back up. The other curls around my waist, clutching gently. "I'm a fan."

I laugh softly, but my chest burns warm at his words. "Thanks, Bryson." We should really start walking again; this park is decent enough, but it's night in New York, after all. "We should get to the street, probably. Never know where you'll get mugged."

Bryson's arms tighten briefly around me at that, then he unwinds them, keeping one arm around my waist. "Yeah, for sure." We walk a short distance in silence, his hand clutching my hip more firmly now, then out of nowhere he says, "I'd never let anything happen to you. I want you to know that."

I reach over and put my hand on top of his on my hip, squeezing his fingers as best I can. "I know."

And I do. He's big and strong and I'm sure his size alone is enough of a deterrent for anyone looking to steal a purse, but self-preservation instincts die hard. Still, he's sweet, and I tell him so.

"Yeah, I'm like sugar, babe," he jokes, as we reach the street. He lets go of me to step onto the road, peering out for a cab. "Where are we going anyway? Home?"

I shrug. "Unless, there's somewhere else you want to go."

Bryson moves his head back and forth, clearly hedging on something. "I know Quinn's at this place uptown, think Bhati is there, too. Want a nightcap?"

He's smiling at me with absolutely no pressure, a reassuring 'whatever you want' expression on his handsome face. Under the streetlights, with his black shirt and his slacks and those light eyes, he looks incredible. I understand the impulse of girls to throw themselves at him. I want him to catch me, too.

"Yeah," I decide, nodding. "Sounds good."

The bar we end up at is crowded - there's definitely some kind of event going on, which explains why Quinn is here - but Quinn and Bishop have managed to snag a booth with some extra room, if we squeeze. Bryson hasn't let go of me since we left the lecture, practically, so I don't think he'll mind the tight fit.

"God damn, Carleigh," Bishop says when we walk up, me holding onto Bryson's hand to not get lost in the crowd. "You look hot. Look at your little waist in that dress!"

"Thanks, Bishop." I've been running a lot, so I've earned that compliment. I take a step up to hoist myself into the tall booth and Bryson slides in beside me. His ears are a little red, too, but before I can ask him if something's wrong, a waitress is on us. I order a vodka and seltzer and Bryson gets a beer; by the time that's through, he's already talking to Bishop's date, a good-looking guy who introduces himself as Paul.

"Can't believe you got him to go to a lecture." Bishop shakes his head. "The guy who used to skip history class."

"Used to skip a lot of classes," Quinn laughs. "Not just history!" He has a mischievous look on his face, but he kind of always does, so I don't know quite what to make of it. "I can see it, though. I'd go anywhere with you in that dress, Carleigh."

Bryson's hand drops unexpectedly onto my lap just then, his palm flattening and then curling around my thigh just where the hem rides up past my knee. "So, Quinn, how's the opening going?" he asks loudly.

"Great," Quinn replies, his eyes flashing with more of that puckish glint from earlier. "Meeting a lot of interesting people."

"That so?"

There's an edge to the way Bryson is speaking that is confusing me. I decide not to try to figure out what's going on with him and Quinn, and instead turn to talk to Paul. I find out he's a consultant for an environmental waste management company, and that he and Bishop met at a bar about a month prior. He's friendly and has nice, kind eyes; I like him for Bishop.

"What about you guys?" Paul asks, nodding toward me and Bryson. "How long have you guys been together?"

"Oh," I say, feeling heat rise in my cheeks and desperately wishing for it to go away. "I, we're not a - Bryson's my roommate."

Paul lifts an eyebrow just slightly. I could be wrong, but I see his eyes flip briefly down to my lap, where from his angle, Bryson's hand placement must be clear. "Oh, my mistake," he says, but there's a quirk to the corner of his lips as he takes a sip of his drink.

Oh no. Not another one of these types in my life - it's the last thing a girl trying to get over a crush on her friend needs. Luckily, the song shifts, and I'm saved by Bishop tugging on Paul's arm. "Let's go dance!"

Paul waves at me and follows Bishop out of the booth. Quinn, who stepped aside to let them exit, slides back in. "So, how's marathon training going, Carleigh?" he asks.

I groan. "Don't remind me about that right now - I've got another twelve miles to do tomorrow."

"It's going good though, right?" Bryson interjects, looking down at me for confirmation. "You seemed pretty happy with your pace yesterday."

I take a long sip of my drink, relishing in the cool liquid, wishing for balance to come to my mind. "Yes," I confirm, speaking quickly after realizing they are both waiting for me. "Yeah, it's going okay. I'm on track for where I want to be. I'd like to do a four-hour marathon, if I can, but I'll be happy with around four and a half. Really anything under five."

"I'm exhausted just thinking about it," Quinn tells me, with a shake of his head.

Bryson chuckles. "Every time she comes back to the apartment, I feel lazier and lazier."

I frown and click my tongue. "Oh, Bryson, come on. You work a physical job. You're in great shape."

"My endurance is shot to hell, though." He shrugs. "But oh well. Some of us are built for strength, not speed! And then some of us are built for neither. Right, Quinn?"

"Oh, that's not what you were saying when I beat your ass outside of-"

"Piss off about that, we were literally kids. Let go of your one victory."

I roll my eyes and swirl a melting cube of ice around my glass. "I'm sure you're both Frank Dux now."

That stalls them both mid-argument. Quinn looks at me, wide-eyed, then at Bryson. "Er, was that a Bloodsport reference?" he asks, surprised.

I shrug and sip my cocktail. "Don't sound so shocked."

Bryson lifts his hand from my leg so he can take mine.

"The perfect woman," he marvels in a teasing tone, eyes twinkling as he gazes at me. "Marry me."

I giggle and tug my hand out of his. "I don't know, Bryson, can you do the splits like Jean-Claude van Damme?"

He slaps his hand on the table jovially. "I'll learn!"

Quinn winces. "Sounds painful, I don't know."

"You saying I'm not worth it?" I ask, laughing.

"You're great, but no way would my body do that," Quinn declares, leaning back in the booth. He surveys us with amusement in his eyes. "And from what I know of him, neither would Bryson's."

"Little bit of yoga would do you both some good," I suggest. "Get to where you can touch your toes."

"Aw, that's not fair," Bryson complains. "I have long legs."

I snort. "Such a victim complex," I tease. "Short people have a lock on the height complaint thing, Bryson. That's our thing. You don't get to have the best view everywhere, the ability to reach anything you want, and get to complain about your height. It just doesn't work that way."

"Sure it does." He drapes his arm around my shoulders. "I got bad knees!"

"Same," Quinn chimes in. They actually clink their beers together at that - weird thing to celebrate, but to each their own.

We stay for a little while longer. Bryson has another beer, but I switch to water. I'll sleep in a little tomorrow, but I need to be able to get up early enough to do my run before it's too hot. I zone out while Bryson and Quinn are talking about something sports-related that I've got no interest in, and stifle a yawn. Just when I'm proud of myself for hiding my tiredness so well, Bryson gets the bill.

"Oh, Bryson, you don't need to leave on my account," I protest. "I can get home just fine by myself."

"Not letting you take the subway home alone at this hour, Carleigh," Bryson says, handing the waitress his credit card.

My eyes roll. His protective streak has reared its head a few times lately; it's sweet, and most of the time, but he's being a little crazy. "Bryson, I take the subway at this hour all the time after work."

"That's different."

I laugh. "What? How is it different?"

"Just is."

I sigh and sit back, waiting for the waitress to return. I look at Quinn, who just raises his palms to me as if to announce he's not going to take a side. "I think you're being a little silly. I can get a cab, if it makes you feel better."

"I'm not, and it doesn't, but it doesn't matter anyway. I'm tired, too, Carleigh."

The waitress returns with a receipt and Bryson's visa. He signs it, then we make our goodnights with Quinn, Bishop, and Paul, and head out through the crowd. Once we get to the street, Bryson moves to peer out at the traffic, hoping to hail a cab. I watch, anxious.

I should drop it. I really, really should drop it. But I'm curious: he's been a little off since we got here, between the brief tension with Quinn to the way his hand held my leg, even to the way that he stiffened up when a friendly, seemingly harmless guy approached our table and offered me a drink. I want to know what's going on.

So, before he can raise a hand to hail a ride, I reach out and brush my fingertips against his forearm. "You okay?"

Bryson turns halfway and looks at me, his blue eyes piercing. "I'm fine. Just trying to get us home."

"I don't think that's true," I say slowly. "You're not usually like this."

He frowns, turning fully toward me now. "Like what?"

I sigh and wave my hands. "Like ... this," I emphasize, gesturing to him. "Overprotective."

Bryson's eyebrows shoot up. "I shouldn't be worried about you going home alone at night?"

"No, that's - well, no! It's fine. I'm fine. I'm a big girl, Bryson. I've done fine for myself on the train for a long time in this city."

"Jesus Christ, Carleigh," Bryson swears, grabbing my wrist. He tugs me to the side, out of earshot of another couple who are standing nearby and giving us an odd look. "I swear to god, you're blind to it. Totally blind to it."

I'm hopelessly confused. "What are you talking about?" He's holding my wrist a little tightly; I tug at it slightly and he drops it, looking briefly apologetic.

"Half the guys in that place were staring at you, Carleigh," Bryson tells me, his voice fierce in a way I haven't heard before. "Jesus, this dress isn't even showing anything and you're the best thing anyone's laid eyes on. And you didn't notice, probably, just like you didn't notice the guy at your bar trying to look down your shirt or the others staring at your ass - and that's just the night I was there! And - fuck," he swears, running a hand through his hair. "I feel like such an idiot, because they all make me so mad, but I'm turning around and doing the same thing."

He turns away from me and takes a few steps down the sidewalk. I can hear him breathing slowly, in and out with audible sighs. I can see him raise a palm and run it over his face, sighing again.

"Bryson," I try, unsure of what to say. I don't understand, still, what his outburst is about. I get hit on with somewhat regular occasions when I'm at work, but it's usually nothing obscene and certainly not cause for him to be concerned about my safety. I made that clear to him weeks ago. "I don't -"

Bryson cuts me off, but he doesn't turn around. "Sorry, Carleigh," he says, his voice almost crumbling. "You're right. I'm being a sexist dick. I know you can take care of yourself."

I walk toward him gingerly. He doesn't move away when I'm right behind him, which I take as a good sign. I put my hands on his back, flattening my palms to soothe his flinch at my touch. Then I slip my arm around his waist and hug him, his back to my front, on the sidewalk.

After a few seconds, I feel Bryson's hands cover mine. He lets out a long breath that sounds almost relieved. "Carleigh?"

My forehead is pressed against his shirt. His back is warm, bordering on damp; he must be hot. "Yeah?"

"I really do want to go home anyway. I promise."

I squeeze him as best as I can. "Then get a cab."

We don't talk about it on the way home.

I'm a curious person, an endless learner, and I have so many questions. I don't understand why Bryson snapped tonight. I've never seen him with that intensity and fire in his eyes, and I've certainly never been on the receiving end of an outburst like that - from anyone, let alone from the most consistently upbeat and cheerful person I know. I want to understand - but he's still acting a little odd when we get home and I don't think it's a good time to ask. Tomorrow, I vow, if he seems more like himself, I'll ask.

I take my shoes off as soon as I get in the door, relishing in the familiar dip of a flat surface on the soles of my feet. I decide to change, and disappear into my bedroom without saying anything to Bryson.

I take off my dress and sit on the edge of my bed in my bra and underwear. I pull my pajama drawer open and stare at my options, uncertain. I'm still so hopelessly confused about Bryson, about what he said.

I play it back in my head. What did that mean? That he has been looking at me? Staring at my ass and whatever else he went rambling on about? It seems impossible; Bryson is the kind of guy who should be dating a six-foot Victoria's Secret model, not a five-foot-four mostly antisocial nerd who likes baking a little too much. He's incredibly out of my league in every way, and the reason I know that is because I've checked him out, too. I'm very aware of his muscled arms, his vibrantly blue eyes, his imperfect smile, his construction crew t-shirt, the way his pants sit on his hips. I live with it every day. If he liked the way I looked in the dress in a way that was more than just friendly, well - that's ... interesting.

I shake the thought from my head. The whole concept is a little beyond the pale as far as believability goes. Still, when I get dressed, the pajamas I instinctively choose are a set I only wear when it's blisteringly hot outside: a pair of shorts printed with doughnuts Trinity got me as a joke, and a white tank top with thin straps. It's not an obscene choice - this isn't a seduction mission, I'm not in the business of intentional failure, after all - but I am probably showing more skin than he's ever seen of me.

I'm just curious.

Bryson has changed, too; he's got a beanie back on his head and is wearing shorts with a t-shirt from a local brewery. He's sitting on the couch with a big bottle of water in front of him, flipping through recommendations on Netflix, and looks up when I walk by on my way to the kitchen.

"I'm kind of hungry," I say by way of greeting, not stopping as I walk. "I'm going to heat up some of those pizza rolls from last week. You want any?"

When I look back for his answer, it's obvious that his eyes are following me. "Sure, Carleigh," he answers, his voice gentle.

"Coming right up." I walk into the kitchen and grab a couple of my frozen pastries from the freezer. I get the idea that grating some fresh parmesan on top will make for a nice crispiness when I stick them in the oven for a quick reheat, so I pull that out of the fridge as well and then open the cupboard where the grater is. "Oh," I comment to myself, noticing it's somehow found its way to the highest shelf. Bryson.

In normal times, I'd ask him for help, but things feel sort of tense and the pizza roll is kind of my peace offering. I could also go grab the folding step stool that has been put away since he moved in, but it's just a quick reach and it hardly seems worth the effort. So instead, I hoist myself onto the counter and shift onto my knees.

"Carleigh, what are you doing?"

My head twists around, hand on the grater, and I see

Bryson standing at the edge of the kitchen with his arms crossed and an amused look on his face.

"You put the grater up high," I complain, lifting it down and setting it on the counter. "I had to improvise."

Bryson walks over to me, shaking his head. "You could have just asked me to grab it." He slides one arm around my abdomen from the back, his hand holding the curve of my waist, supports my legs with his other arm, then sweeps me off the counter with ease. "You're going to hurt yourself before your race."

I hold onto his arm as he sets my feet on the floor. He doesn't let go of me immediately, and now I'm standing on the ground, very aware that my breasts are brushing against his forearm. "You looked relaxed on the couch," I lie. "Didn't want to bug you."

Bryson's arm loosens, but doesn't entirely drop. I turn against it so I'm facing him now, and I can see another unreadable expression on his face. I'm not so sure I like this version of Bryson, emotionally - he's usually such an open book, so upbeat when things are good and so obvious when something bad has happened. The lack of clarity is bothering me.

"You aren't bugging me," he says softly. His arm drops to my hip. His hand is so big that it stretches almost the whole length of my little shorts. His fingers curl around the side of my hip so far that half of his hand is essentially on my ass; it's all I can notice. His thumb presses into my hip bone, rubbing gently. "Doughnuts, huh?" he asks.

I smile and look down at my shorts. "They were a gift," I tell him. "I went through a real homemade doughnut phase, and Trinity thought they were funny."

"Roommate gifts!" Bryson says, his voice louder now and approaching some degree of normalcy, even as we stand here in this very not-normal position. "I'll have to get you some, too, I guess. Pickles, maybe sauerkraut."

"Pickles," I tease, squeezing his bicep. "Very Bryson."

"Very you, Half-Sour." He lets his hands fall and steps away from me. "So, what are gratin'?" he asks.

I point to the cheese on the counter. "Parm for the top of the rolls," I say. "Now that you're here, you can do it!"

"Always putting me to work," Bryson comments with a smile, picking up the grater and the block of cheese. "Your wish is my command."

The parmesan turns out to be a great idea. It crisps up nicely under the broiler and adds a good texture. When I'm done eating, I set my empty plate on the coffee table and settle back on the couch next to Bryson, who finished minutes prior.

"Perfect late-night snack," he declares.

"Agreed." I fold my hands in my lap and glance over at him. He's tired, too; I can see it in his face. And yet still, I can't seem to shake the feeling that something is off between them.

Despite my better instincts, I do what's been ingrained into me for years: I apologize.

"Hey, Bryson?"

His eyes are closed. "Mhm."

"I'm sorry. About earlier." His eyes snap open and he sits up, but I continue. "I don't really know what happened tonight, but it felt kind of weird and tense. If there's something I did, I'm sorry."

Bryson sighs and drops his face into his hands, briefly

rubbing it before lifting his head again to look at me. "You didn't do anything, don't apologize. I'm the asshole who - I need to do a better job of handling my own shit."

"But I don't understand," I say, probing his knee with my fingertips. "What does that mean?"

"Nothing," he tells me. "I'm trying to work through something in my head and I got you all caught up in it, that's all."

I press my lips together. I'm dissatisfied, but he obviously isn't in the mood to get into it, so I'll stop. "Is there anything I can do to help?"

Bryson shakes his head. "It's all good."

I sigh, but ultimately nod. "Okay, but you can talk to me, Bryson. About anything you want. You know that, right?"

He smiles, warm and genuine, and in that moment it's like tonight never happened. "Yeah, Carleigh," he answers. "I know." He extends his arm toward me. "Come here. I need a Carleigh-bear."

I chuckle and scoot toward him, my laughter turning to a giggle when he hauls me into his lap. I hug him, feeling tall from my new perch on his thighs, and melt as his arms wind around me in return. It's warm and cozy here, and I'm so tired; I rest my head over his shoulder and relax, thinking I could fall asleep if he let me.

Logically, I know this isn't normal. I know that two friends shouldn't be sitting like this. I shouldn't be clutching onto him, tracing circles into the back of his neck with my fingernail, and he shouldn't be holding the twist of my waist with his palm the way that he is. But we are, and it feels natural, comfortable, so when his left hand slides down my back and hooks under my thigh to hold me closer, I let him. I let his hand rub back and forth between my thigh and hip, let his palm curve around my ass, and I pretend not to notice something twitching ever-so-slightly beneath me. I thread my fingers into his curls at the back of his head, press a closed-mouth kiss to the side of his neck, and exhale in time with him, long and slow.

I don't count how long I sit there in his arms; time doesn't really seem to move at the same rate, anyway. Finally, I break the hug and lean back a bit in his arms. "I should go to bed," I say, apologies in my voice.

Bryson's eyes are searching mine, a darker blue than normal, but still as beautiful as they always are. "Same," he says. My shirt has shifted in our embrace, the top of it slightly askew, and when he squeezes my ribcage his thumb rubs against the side of my right breast. "You really did look beautiful tonight," he says softly, his thumb still stroking. "Sorry, I was a dick about it after."

I can't take this much longer; I'm going to combust soon if he doesn't stop, if I don't move, if we don't part and go to bed. And I'm not ready to ruin a good thing. Not yet. "Water under the bridge," I dismiss. "You looked good, too." I lean forward and kiss his cheek, trying to ignore the brief, fleeting sensation of my breast pressing more fully into his hand. Finally, I pull away and slide off him, standing up. "Goodnight, Bryson."

"Night, Carleigh," he echoes.

14

BRYSON

I have this idea at the end of July.

Initially, all I wanted was to support Carleigh. Sure, I'm attracted to her, and have been, but it didn't seem mutual. So, I just want to be a good friend and friends support each other, cheer each other on - and what more reason to do that than when they run a marathon?

The rundown is that the marathon she signed up for is the full marathon at Lake Placid, about five hours away from the city. Just showing up isn't going to be as simple as if it were in Brooklyn or Queens. But I've been to the Adirondacks before and have always had a great time, so even if everything else backfires, I'll at least be in a beautiful place, right? So, toward the end of the month, I pulled the trigger and organized a surprise camping trip with some friends so that we could be there to cheer her on. Even if she is too tired to stay after and feels like going back to the city, she will appreciate us showing up.

Then, not even a week later, that night happened. The

night where I went to her school's event and then acted like a jackass, because I couldn't stop feeling jealous and protective every time someone glanced her way with anything but platonic interest. The night where I almost ruined everything inside some new hipster bar that won't be open a month from now.

I have no idea what it is about Carleigh that drives me so crazy, because I've never felt quite this erratic before with any other girl, but I almost blew it. It took all of my self-control at that bar not to grab her and kiss her and tell her that I want her to be mine, and only mine - and in the end, I hadn't even really controlled myself, given that I ended up kind of yelling at her on the sidewalk.

But then - then we went home, and things had gotten ... muddy. Carleigh came out of her bedroom wearing a little pajama set she had to know was going to draw my eye, then she smiled at me with those big beautiful eyes, hugged and touched me, pulled my hair and kissed my neck. She'd let me drag my big clumsy hands over her runner's legs and her perfect ass, and pretty sure that if I moved to palm her perky breasts, she'd have let me do that, too.

Now, I have no idea what's going on between us. We're not just friends, we're not quite more, either. We haven't talked about it since that night - Carleigh tried a little when we returned home from the bar, but for all of the signals that it may be mutual, I'm not confident, and just not ready to face that overt rejection. Not from someone I want to keep in my life, regardless of what role she plays.

The two weeks since that night have been busy. She's had a lot going on at school, not to mention trying to rest and stay healthy and be prepared for her run. Plus, now I'm back at work and experienced a few hard days. But now, before I go to bed, I always offer a hug, and she always accepts. But nothing like that night has happened again.

The night before Carleigh is set to leave for Lake Placid, though, feels different. Her parents are coming to watch from Boston, and they've booked a hotel for the three of them for the night before. Carleigh has no idea that Quinn, Molly, Bishop, and Sawyer and I are leaving almost immediately after she is. She doesn't know Molly is coming over the next morning to pack her a few extra days' worth of clothes, just in case she wants to stay with us into next week, and she doesn't know when she crosses the finish line, we'll all be there to pat her on the back. Her parents do, apparently – I've never met or talked to them, but Molly passed the plan along just in case.

Nope; as far as Carleigh knows, she's getting a ride up with a running buddy who's also doing the marathon, meeting her parents, doing the actual marathon, then heading back the same way. And she's nervous.

"You're going to do great, Carleigh," I say encouragingly, nudging her half-eaten bowl of pasta toward her. "You have to fuel up."

She shakes her head and groans, flopping back onto the couch dramatically. "What if I've been doing all this running for six months and I get there and I fall in the first mile? And I break my leg and I can't finish and -"

"Carleigh," I cut in gently, laughing despite the cross look she gives me. "None of that's going to happen."

"What if it does?"

I pat her hand reassuringly. "It won't."

Carleigh sighs. She peers at her pasta and then pushes it

away. "I can't finish this," she whines. "I'm too anxious." Her eyes flick to me. "Can I - I could use a hug," she asks lamely.

I smile at her and open my arm. "Anytime, Carleigh, you don't have to ask."

Carleigh exhales and shuffles to me on her knees, leaning over a bit until she can slip her arms around my neck. I gently reach over and pull her by her hip until she falls to sit on my lap. Immediately, her arms tighten around me. I put mine around her, too, holding her close and feeling her breathe in and out slowly, calming herself down. She's dressed pretty casually today, in a blue t-shirt that's clearly from a vacation to the Grand Canyon and a pair of gray sweatpants, but a few inches of her lower back are exposed by the way she's sitting, and I take the opportunity to slide my palms against her skin.

"I can't wait for this to be over," she mumbles over my shoulder. "The training's been fun, and I like the challenge, but I'm just tired."

I rub her back. "You've been working hard," I agree. "Think how good it'll be to sleep in the day after."

"Mm." She presses her face into my t-shirt. "That feels good, Bryson."

I increase the pressure a little. "Like that?"

Carleigh nods. "Yeah." She reaches around and pushes my hand higher. "Can you - right between my shoulder blades-"

"Oh - yeah, sure." My hand drifts past the rough lace and hard satin of her bra and dig in the center of her upper back, pushing against her, and at the same time, pulling her body even more toward mine. She whines a little - a good noise, I think - then her muscles soften, and I notice her relax.

I pull back and turn her upper body to the side, readjusting so she's sitting on my right leg and leaning the left side of her body against my chest, her left hand in her own lap and her head next to mine. "I swear, Bryson," she sighs, "you missed your calling as a massage therapist. Or a baker. Would've done great at either with strong hands like that."

I chuckle. "What do I need to be a baker for, Carleigh?" My right hand, now resting lazily against her hip, slides up slightly and tickles her stomach. "I got you."

She shrieks; she's incredibly ticklish, something I learned weeks ago, and it's adorable as hell when she laughs. She pushes at my hand and tries to wiggle away, but I grab her around the middle and pull her back, tickling her again until she gasps, "I give up, I give up!" and hits my hands with her palms.

I obediently stop tickling, but I don't move my arms from where they are, now locked around her waist, each hand holding the opposite curve. She slumps against me.

"You going to let me go?" she asks, when she catches her breath.

I shrug. "I'll think about it," I tease. "For now, I think I'll just keep you trapped here."

Carleigh sighs. "Fine," she concedes, and for a minute I think I've won. But then, she starts wiggling her hips rhythmically, back and forth, and god damn her, she's teasing me and trying to get me worked up enough that I'll let her go, and it's definitely working.

"You're a little devil," I tell her, as I release her.

She giggles. She's free now, but she doesn't move off of my lap. I desperately want to read into this.

"Sorry," she says, not sounding apologetic at all as she

relaxes into me, tucking her knees toward her, but the roll of her ass over my one leg sends an unpleasant pain into my femur and I swear under my breath. Carleigh sits up immediately. "Oh no, I hurt you," she frets, trying to pull her legs toward the floor so she can get off me. "I knew I was too heavy, Bryson, you should've said I was too heavy-"

"Give me a break, Carleigh, you're basically a doll. I told you, I got bad knees!" I readjust and gesture for her to come back. She looks at me dubiously. "Come here."

"No way," she refuses, shaking her head. "I almost broke your leg."

I roll my eyes. "Oh my god, no you didn't." I sigh; it's been two weeks, and I just really - I really want to hold her again. "Will you lay with me?" I ask. "If I lay down, will you lay with me?"

Carleigh's eyes are soft when she looks at me. "Yeah, okay," she says quietly. "But if I hurt you-"

"I'll tell you," I assure her, scooting my big ass down on the couch until I'm laying down - as much as I'll fit, anyway; my shoulders and head are propped up against the arm so that my legs will fit on as well. Carleigh then gingerly places a knee between mine, brackets her other leg around mine, and lowers herself down until her head is on my chest and her arms are on either side of me. Our hips are aligned in this position - I hadn't quite considered that, that could be a problem - but otherwise, she fits perfectly, feels perfect, like a pretty weighted blanket, melting my anxieties away.

Carleigh's left hand rests on my bicep. My muscles are sore, still adjusting to being back at work after having been away for a short while, but her hand is delicate, and so pale against my more tanned skin. Her nails scratch lightly, which feels amazing.

Christ. I think I might love her.

"Carleigh, I'm warning you, I think I might fall asleep."

"Mm." Her thumb rubs my arm. "It's alright. Me, too."

"Catnap?" I suggest, and when she nods, I turn off the TV. It's only seven o'clock, but our apartment faces east and it's dark in the evenings, even now. I close my eyes, feeling my chest rise and fall and her along with it, then sleep comes.

We wake up spooning.

I'm not even sure how, logistically. The couch is not large enough for both of us to comfortably sleep here. But here we are, doing it anyway: she's tucked in front of me, with one of her legs kicked back between my thighs and the other bent to match mine - as best as she can, anyway, considering our height difference. My right arm is bent, my own head in my palm, hers resting on my bicep; my left arm is wrapped tightly around her abdomen, palm curved around so far that my knuckles are pressing against the couch.

It's only seven, but it's darker still in our apartment, and for a minute I consider just closing my eyes again and sleeping until morning. But she hasn't finished packing, and I have texts to send and arrangements of my own to finalize. I nudge the back of her shoulder with my chin, over the thick fabric of her shirt. "Carleigh, babe - wake up," I whisper.

"No," she whines, turning her face into my arm. "I don't want to."

I smile; she's so cute. "You have to finish packing."

"Oh." Carleigh turns around, somehow managing to stay

on the couch, and slips her right knee between mine. She buries her face in my t-shirt, as if she's able to get deep enough into me, she can hide forever. "You're the worst alarm clock ever."

I laugh softly and grab her hip, so she doesn't fall off of the couch. "No, there has to be worse alarms than me." Then, feeling daring, I reach down, grab her ass with my open palm, and smack it. "Up and at 'em!"

Her eyes fly open. "Bryson!" Carleigh yelps, giggling as she reaches around to the edge of the couch and sits up. "Oh my god."

"Worked, didn't it?" I shrug, winking at her.

Carleigh stands up and flips her middle finger. "Fine, fine, I'll go finish packing." She gives a heavy sigh, one that I recognize: it's the same one I breathe whenever I have to go do something I don't want to.

I clear my throat. "Hey, Carleigh?"

She stops before turning the corner into the hallway. "Yeah?"

"You're going to do great," I tell her. "Don't worry."

Carleigh smiles. "Thanks," she says, then she's gone.

15

BRYSON

I'm not really a planner. I know how best to keep a kitchen arranged, have a preference for the way I like my hunting stuff to be stored in my mom's garage, and have a system for my tackle box. But planning - not exactly my strong suit, not really.

But for this trip to Lake Placid to support Carleigh in her marathon efforts, I really pulled out all the stops. I already got everyone lined up to come. Everyone's got stuff they're responsible for bringing. We have sites booked at Saranac Lake - sure, it's about fifteen minutes away by car from Lake Placid, but it's a great area and the drive will be nice. The actual townsite is overrated, anyway; I'll go because it's where the marathon starts and ends, but it's overly commercialized and nothing about it is really camping, not by my definition.

This won't be, either; we've got tents and are bringing food, sure, but we won't be digging holes in the woods for latrines, and there are places to shower if people need. I'm a fan of a more back-woods style of camping, where you wander into the wilderness with your supplies and emerge two weeks later - reeking, but having had the time of your life, with your garbage bundled on your back so that Mother Nature couldn't tell you were even there. This isn't that, not at all, but it'll be more relaxed, too. Relieving oneself in the woods isn't for everybody.

Carleigh leaves fairly early in the morning. I'm awake, wearing pajama pants, and a t-shirt, pretending to have rolled out of bed just to say goodbye. It's the day before her marathon; she's heading up to have a good night's sleep at a hotel with her parents, then she'll start the run early in the morning. The plan on my end is that myself, Molly, and Quinn will drive up together in a few hours, with Bishop and Sawyer just behind us. We'll set up our campsite and get prepared for a long morning of marathon-watching the next day, then spend a few days hiking, canoeing, and generally having a good time in the great outdoors. It's going to be great.

Of course, Carleigh knows none of this, so I make sure to be out of my room to wish her luck when she leaves. I give her a hug. "Knock 'em dead, Half-Sour," I say, pressing a light kiss to her temple. "Run like the wind. And text me when you're done to let me know how it went."

Carleigh nods. "Will do," she says, heading through the doorway with her bag. She gives a nervous smile, waves, then lets the door shut.

Immediately, I hop into gear: Molly's coming over soon to pack up a bag for Carleigh, so I have to hop in the shower.

My own stuff is mostly packed, but I'll do a last check, and also leave time to head to Jersey so that I can pick up my dad's old truck and most of our camping supplies. It's a hectic morning and it's going to be a long drive up, but it'll be worth it when Carleigh sees all of our faces at the finish line. I know it will.

∽

I WAKE to the sound of birds chirping, feeling great. Obviously, part of this is because I get to see Carleigh right away, which really is kind of stupid, because I live with Carleigh, and see her all the time. I saw her yesterday. But screw it – I've got a thing for her and seeing her makes me happy. So, sue me. However, another big reason I feel great is because I'm lying in a warm sleeping bag, inside the new one-man tent I recently bought in a March off-season sale, my head on my best compressible pillow, outdoors.

I love the outdoors, sleeping under the stars, telling stories by a campfire and hanging out by the cold waters of a lake. I love it all. It's impossible to feel less than amazing when you're in nature - at least for me, and especially if you normally live in a gigantic, busy city like New York.

I check my watch. Carleigh's run starts at eight, before it gets too hot, and I want to be there to see Carleigh off - if we could find her. It's six now, so I decide to pull myself out of the sleeping bag and start percolating coffee.

It works; around six-fifteen, Molly and Sawyer emerge from the four-man tent that they are sharing, and five minutes after that, Bishop and Quinn appear from theirs.

Everyone has a cup of campfire coffee, then get ready and head out to Lake Placid, with the promise of actual coffee and food from one of the cafes in the townsite at the top of their minds.

The run at Lake Placid is, apparently, incredibly popular; it's very crowded in town, so Bishop has to park his car far away. As we walk toward the old Olympic speed skating oval, where the race starts, Molly has her phone out and is texting Carleigh's mother.

"They're over by a big purple sign, apparently," she reports, sliding her phone into the back pocket of her shorts. She wrings her hands together and grins at me as we walk. "Oh, I'm excited now!"

I laugh. "Think she'll be happy to see us?"

Molly gives me a look. "She's going to be thrilled, Bryson. Wouldn't you be?"

"I'd be pumped as hell," Quinn interjects. "Big purple sign, huh? Is it that one?" He points east, through the mill of runners and supports, to where a large purple-colored sign is advertising in-town parking spots.

Molly stands on her toes. "I see them, I see Carleigh's dad. Come on."

I'm not sure what Carleigh's parents look like, so I don't really have a grasp on where we're headed, but as I follow in line behind Bishop, Molly, Sawyer, and Quinn, I finally see Carleigh. She's standing with an older man and woman - yeah they definitely look like they could be her parents - and has a racing bib pinned to her tank top.

"Carleigh!" Molly yells, jumping and waving her hand. We're still a few feet away, but her voice must carry well enough, because Carleigh turns our way and squints, curiously.

I see a look of recognition cross her face as she spots us. "Molly?" she says, holding one hand over her eyes to shield the sun. "What are you - Bryson?"

We push through the last block of people separating us from Carleigh. She hugs Molly tightly. "What are you guys doing here?"

"We came to cheer you on, dummy," Molly says, hugging her back. She raises her eyebrow at Carleigh and then gestures toward me. "It was your roommate's idea."

Carleigh looks over at me with a look of what almost seems like awe as she hugs Quinn, Sawyer, and then Bishop in succession. "I can't believe you guys came," she says, shaking her head at Sawyer.

"Wouldn't have missed it!" Bishop tells her, flashing his brilliant white grin.

When Carleigh reaches me, she stands in front of me for an extra moment. "Bryson, I - you did this?"

"Didn't think I was going to settle for just a text after, did you?" I tease, stepping forward for a hug. "Wanted to surprise you."

She practically jumps onto me and stands on the toes of her broken-in running shoes so she can wind her arms around my neck. I hug her tightly, squeezing her waist affectionately, but not letting myself indulge. After all, I can see her parents a few feet away. Molly has gone over to talk to them, but her mother is definitely looking over at Carleigh still.

She pulls back and looks up at me with unshed tears

shining in her big eyes. "I can't believe you didn't tell me you guys were coming!" she exclaims, hitting my arm.

"That's the surprise part," Quinn jokes, which earns an eye roll from Carleigh.

"Thanks, Quinn, very helpful explanation."

"Anytime!" Quinn replies cheerfully.

I rub her upper back between her shoulder blades, where I know she's been sore. "So, how are you feeling? Good? Ready?"

Carleigh nods, sniffing a little. She swipes at her eyes. "Nervous, but I feel a lot better now that you guys are here." She leans into me, hugging my side. "I'm ready to get it done."

I tilt my head down to whisper in her ear. "You've got this. I just know it."

She nods and looks up. "Your optimism is appreciated, Bryson." Then a look of realization dawns on her face. "Sorry, I'm being so rude. You guys, come meet my parents." She leads us over to where Molly is standing, and gestures to the two older people. "These are my parents, Jay and Monica"

"I'm Bishop," Bishop says, shaking both of their hands.

Quinn's next. "And you are…"

"Jackson," Quinn answers, moving onto shaking Carleigh's dad's hand. "Nice to meet both of you."

Sawyer introduces herself next, then steps aside so the line of introductions can more easily continue; she gestures to me that she's going to grab a race map from a nearby stand, and heads over with Molly.

I smile at Carleigh's mom as she approaches me. "Hi ma'am, I'm-"

"Bryson," she finishes, looking at Carleigh. "We've heard lots about you."

"That so?" I look at Carleigh with a wide grin; she rolls her eyes and waves her hand.

Carleigh's dad introduces himself to me as well. "Nice to meet you, son," he says. "Good of you to come cheer on our Carleigh."

I smile good-naturedly. "Well, I see her in and out all the time prepping for this - figured I couldn't miss the main event! Plus this place is great, I love the area, so that doesn't hurt either."

Molly walks over with Sawyer close behind, both now holding race maps. "Okay, Carleigh - I think we picked out a couple places that we can hopefully wait around to catch you along the way."

I check my watch. It's nearly time to start; she should be heading over. Carleigh seems to realize this at the same time as I do, because she checks the runners' watch on her right wrist and groans nervously.

"You're going to do great, sweetheart," Carleigh's father tells her. "We'll all be cheering you on. Maybe your mother will end up buying more of those damn ornamental plates - there's a boutique in town here."

Monica rolls her eyes at her husband. "I just said I wanted to look." She gives Carleigh a hug. "Good luck, honey."

"Thanks, Mom. Thanks, Dad." Carleigh rocks back and forth on her heels. "Okay," she says, taking a deep breath. "Heading over. See you guys after, I hope?" she asks, her eyes finding mine.

I smile at her and nod. "We'll be here, Carleigh. Knock 'em dead!"

"I'll do my best." She turns and heads over to the starting line.

The seven of us move up to a better spot along the early course, standing with the rest of the spectators. Quinn and I move to stand toward the side, both conscious as always of the fact that we're definitely blocking people behind us from seeing. We cheer once the starting gun goes off, clapping and hollering alongside everybody else, then find Carleigh's parents and our shorter friends again.

"Well kids, I think we're going to look around the town a bit," Monica tells them. "I'm sure we'll see you all around later." She gives me a pointed look. I give a friendly wave in response, not knowing what else to do, but once Carleigh's parents are out of earshot, I turn to Molly.

"Did you see that look she gave me?" I ask. "What was that about?"

Molly yawns. "Probably just letting you know that she knows that you're very clearly super in love with her daughter."

My jaw falls open. "I - what?" My face is heating up. I can take this from Quinn, but Molly? Thankfully, the rest of our friends have already started walking toward a coffee shop, and Molly and I are bringing up the rear, so there's no indication that any of them overheard.

Molly looks almost bored by the conversation. "Are we still pretending that you're not into Carleigh? Come on, Bryson, I've got eyes."

"I'm - I didn't -"

"Hey, I support it." She holds her hands up in surrender.

"She's a lot more relaxed since you moved in, and she seems happier. Well, as relaxed as Carleigh can get, you know. She really, really needs more of that in her life. So, you have my endorsement." We reach the door of the coffee shop; Molly lets out a loud, "Oh, this smells so good, I hope they have bagels."

∽

A LITTLE UNDER four hours later, once we've grabbed food, walked around the town, seen some of the Olympic sites, and loaded a few more groceries into Bishop's car, now it's time to head to the finish line. We managed to snag glimpses of Carleigh at the seven- and nineteen-mile marks; she'd been doing well, running at a decent pace, and on track for what I know her goals are. I hope the final miles have also been good to her, because she's been working so hard and if she comes in over five hours, she'll be disappointed in herself.

Carleigh's parents are there when me, Sawyer, Molly, Bishop, and Quinn arrive. They report that they saw Carleigh not long ago at the twenty-three-mile mark, and it shouldn't be long before she arrives. I check my watch and am happy to see that it means she'll make a great time. I scan the arriving runners, watching person after person slip across the line.

"They all look exhausted," Molly comments. "This is weird, self-inflicted torture."

Carleigh's father laughs. "Yes. Perfect for Carleigh. She never met a challenge she didn't like."

At a distance, I think I see her. The person - definitely a

woman - is wearing the same fuchsia colored tank top as Carleigh. As the blur nears, I can see a bit more clearly, and - yes. "It's Carleigh!" I say loudly, pointing. "Coming right up. Come on, Carleigh!"

The rest of them begin cheering as well as she approaches down the last half-mile. She looks tired, but there's a look of determination on her face that is unmistakable. She won't be defeated, my Carleigh - not by a marathon and not by herself.

She spots us as she nears the finish line, all yelling and cheering for her, and she waves excitedly. Our group hurries over to meet her, and when we get close, Carleigh's father gives me a little push on my back.

"Go on, Bryson. She'll be excited to see you," he says.

Carleigh's a few feet away now, and when she crosses the finish line, her arms lift in victory. Molly and Carleigh's mother are both taking pictures, still yelling excitedly; behind them, Sawyer, Quinn, and Bishop are clapping. I step out into the road, waving at her, and when she gets close enough Carleigh essentially collapses into my arms.

I hold her up easily, my arms solid around her waist and shoulders, and squeeze tightly. "You did so amazing, Carleigh," I say. "I'm so proud of you, you did it!"

She's still panting, her chest heaving to catch her breath from the last burst of energy she'd put through to cross the line. I can feel her nodding against me. "What was the time?" she asks breathlessly.

"4:18-something," Molly pipes in. "They'll have the official times if we go check."

Carleigh smiles at her and let's go of me to give Molly a

hug. "Sorry, I'm so sweaty and vile," she apologizes, as she makes her way down the line.

Carleigh's father produces a modest bouquet of flowers, which he hands to her when she reaches him. "Congrats, sweetheart. You set your mind to it and you did it."

"Oh Dad, you shouldn't have." Carleigh gives him a quick hug. "I need - can we migrate to the food tent? I need a banana or something." She turns, scanning the group of us, and exhales when her eyes fall on me. "I still can't believe you guys are here. It means so much, it really helped. When I was running, all I could think of was that you were all here, and that if I just kept going, I'd get to see you all."

"We wouldn't have missed it for the world, Carleigh," Sawyer says. "Though I have to say, now that I've been here, I don't know if a marathon is in my future."

"Oh no, Sawyer, you have to," Carleigh says, falling in line beside her as we all walk over to where several baskets of fruit and sandwiches and water are set up for the runners. They talk shop for a little while - Sawyer, apparently, has been looking into doing something like this as well - and Carleigh gives us all a bit of a play-by-play in between bites of banana and watermelon.

Eventually, Carleigh looks over at her parents. "I should go take a shower and pack up my stuff before you have to check out of the hotel, huh?"

Her father is looking at his watch. "I hate to break up the party, but - yes, it's getting to be time for us to go."

Carleigh looks over at the group of them. "Where are you guys staying?"

"We're camping at Saranac, fifteen minutes away," Quinn answers.

"And so are you - if you want," Molly adds. "Bryson let me into your room, and I packed you a little bag, if you want to stay with us. We're here 'til Wednesday morning. We've got everything else - food, an extra sleeping bag, the works."

"No pressure though," I interrupt, meeting her eyes to let her know that it's fine if she doesn't want to. "It'll be a lot of fun, but if you want to just head back to the city and relax, that's also-"

"No," she breathes, shaking her head. "No, I'll stay."

16

CARLEIGH

If I hadn't already been pretty sure that I was at least a little in love with Bryson, this – him organizing a group of people to come and cheer me on during the marathon I signed up to run even before I knew him, just to be supportive – solidified it.

But he did, and so now I've just fallen harder for my tall, scruffy, too-loud roommate, who has a knack for airlock jars and who doesn't like to wear shoes. He's impulsive, bright, and probably has mild attention deficit disorder and I'm so, so, so into him.

When my eyes met his, standing there with Molly and all of the others that morning before my run, I was so touched that my heart felt like it almost physically hurt. If my parents and our friends hadn't also been right there, I probably would've kissed him. I settled for a hug, but my mother had given me a knowing look afterward. I can never hide from her. It probably doesn't help that I've definitely talked a little too much about Bryson during our weekly calls; it's all just getting so hard to contain.

And finally, with this gesture, I'm fairly certain it's mutual.

We're at a campsite at a lake a little ways down the highway from Lake Placid. The place is decked out with everything I imagine we could need, including a couple of different cast iron options for cooking over the fire, a coffee press, and lots of food and drinks. There are also three tents – one tiny one that apparently belongs to Bryson, another for Bishop and Quinn, and a larger one for the three girls to share. I'm in here now with Molly, going through the bag she packed for me. Outside, the guys are playing beer darts with Sawyer, and judging by her happy shriek, she's just won.

Overall, Molly has done a decent job. It's my standard summer fare – tank tops, shorts, and a couple of different footwear choices. "I can't believe you guys did this still," I say to Molly, as she pulls out a beach towel. "Where'd you get all the gear out there?"

"Bryson, mostly," Molly answers. "Quinn for a little bit of it. But mainly Bryson. He's like a real woodsman."

"That fits," I reply, and we both giggle. Then, I pull out what is unmistakably the top to a bikini, a bikini that I only own in the first place because of Molly and Trinity, and I groan. "Molly."

She looks completely unfazed. "Carleigh don't make that face, it's like, the most conservative bikini ever. You look incredible and you should show it off. And hey, if Bryson happens to notice, it's not like that'd be the worst thing in the – ouch!" She rubs her arm where I swatted it.

"Shh," I hiss. "Announce it to the whole place, why don't you-"

"Er, you guys making googly eyes at each other every time you're around one another is basically an announcement in and of itself." Molly holds up the bikini top. "We're going to go to the beach tomorrow," she says pointedly.

Before I can think of a suitable retort, Bryson's voice calls out, "Carleigh!"

I poke my head out of the tent, glad for the break. "Yeah?"

"I have to take the truck to load up with wood. You want to help?"

Molly waggles her eyebrows at me and makes a crude gesture with her hands. I give her the finger, then call back, "Yeah, I'll help!"

Before I can leave the tent, Molly reaches out and grabs my wrist. "Hey. I know I'm teasing, but for real, he planned this over a month ago, and he's been so excited. Think about what that means."

I chew my bottom lip, nod, then leave the tent. Bryson strides up to the truck, swinging the keys on one finger as he whistles cheerfully. He seems so happy and at ease; being outside seems to really agree with him. It's so cute I don't even bother to suppress a light laugh.

"What?" he asks, grinning as he hops in the truck.

I climb in the passenger side. "Nothing," I say truthfully, buckling the seatbelt. "You just look like you're really in your element."

"Er, yeah." Bryson pulls out of the site slowly. "What's not to love about this? Trees, friends, fresh air – it's all the best!"

"It is nice," I agree, my fingers tapping restlessly against my leg. It's beautiful, yes – but honestly, while I'm looking forward to this surprise trip, a part of me also wants to be back in our apartment, where I could crawl into his lap and he could hold me, and maybe I would finally kiss him.

When we get to the woodpile, Bryson backs the truck up. I hop out and begin to root through for dry, good pieces. I carry a few to the truck and Bryson takes them from me, looking amused.

"What?"

He smiles and shakes his head. "No, nothing – you don't actually have to help. It doesn't need to be a two-person job."

I'm confused. "You asked me to come help," I remind him, but I lift myself up and sit on the tailgate. I watch as he walks over to the pile and picks up a big armful of wood, his muscles flexing – god, I'm basic, but I find it unbelievably attractive how strong he is.

Bryson sets it all down in the truck bed. As he unloads, he says, "I just wanted an excuse to talk to you." He brushes wood shavings off his t-shirt and looks at me. "We kind of sprung this whole thing on you and I wanted to make sure it was actually okay."

He's sugar, I think immediately. And I've always loved dessert.

"Bryson," I say, smiling. I gesture for him, and he moves to stand in front of my knees, placing two big palms on them. "It's incredible," I reassure him. "It's a very, very good surprise."

Bryson squeezes my kneecaps. "Yeah?"

"Yeah." I scoot forward and reach out for a hug, parting my knees so he can stand between my legs and be closer. His arms come around me and he surrounds me like always, all him and his earthy scent. He's so warm, so calming. It's like a drug.

"Real proud of you, Carleigh," Bryson says into my hair. "Knew you could do it."

"I'm so glad you came," I say softly. "I wanted you to come, but it's so far away, it felt stupid to ask."

Bryson pulls back and smiles down at me with his deeply blue eyes. They twinkle in the sunlight. "Anything for you, Carleigh."

I swallow, and search his face, lifting one hand from his arm to carefully trace the edge of his jaw. He's really handsome, and masculine in a way I never expected to be so into. I can't believe this guy is also so kind, funny and smart, the guy that charmed both my stuffy lit professors and my coolest friends, who's looked out for me since before we were even friends. *God, I want him.*

"Never?" I ask, my voice almost a whisper.

Bryson is looking at me intensely, and right now it's just the two of us, here by this truck and this woodpile. No one else exists. "Carleigh," he says, his voice ragged.

My hand cups the side of his face. I tilt my head up slightly and lean forward, then, like a prayer into the wind, I kiss him softly.

It lasts only a second, and when I pull back he's staring at me, expression unreadable.

There's a moment of silence, with only a bird chirping and the wind in the trees, where I think I've misread the entire last few months. Then his hands grip my hips, haul me forward, and we're kissing again.

The kiss is intense, but gentle in the same way that Bryson is, careful, yet all-in. I hook my right leg over the back of his thigh, tugging him toward me. His hand slides around from my right hip, up the side of my thigh and over to roughly palm at my ass. I groan into his mouth, parting my lips, and he uses it as an opportunity to deepen the kiss.

My hands slide over his biceps, squeezing his muscles, until I'm grasping at his shoulders. He lifts me off of the tailgate like I weigh nothing, supporting me with his hands at the back of my thighs, and I wrap my other leg around him, too. If we weren't in public right now, I would have half a mind to let go of him and lay myself flat on the truck bed; it's the perfect height for him to fuck me like this; rough and wild like I think he might be.

But I'm Carleigh, and he's Bryson, and I want more than for it to be like that right now. I need something different. I break the kiss, breathing heavily for not the first time today, and hug his neck so tightly, that I might compromise his air supply.

He's with me, of course, in sync like usual. He sets me down on the tailgate again, but he still holds me close, his grip firm and secure on my hips and my back, until my breathing settles.

Bryson grips the side of my ribs with his right hand. This time, I'm fairly certain that his thumb rubbing the side of my breast is entirely intentional. "Wow, Carleigh," he breathes, his eyes almost closed.

"Yeah," I agree, staring at the faded gray of his t-shirt. "Wow." I flick my eyes up nervously to his face. "Hey Bryson?"

His eyes open. "Yeah?"

I lean up and kiss him again, delicately this time. "Thank

you. It's the nicest thing anyone's ever done for me," I say softly.

Bryson's big hand shifts on my side and his thumb brushes over my nipple. The pressure is ever-so-slight through the layers of my shirt and bra, but it feels incredible all the same. "I really like you, Carleigh," he says, leaning in to press another kiss to my mouth. "I like you so much I think I might fall apart."

"Bryson," I breathe, feeling the beginnings of a familiar coiling sensation between my legs as his thumb makes another pass. "Me, too."

"Thank god," he says, giving a heavy exhale. His head lifts and he seems to realize where we are, because then he abruptly moves his hand to my leg, clears his throat and says, "Jesus Christ, Carleigh, I'm sorry – just wanted to kiss you and here I am feeling you up right here where anyone could see."

He's making good points. "I didn't mind," I say, feeling almost shy, but yes. Public groping is bad. "But yeah, maybe – maybe not here."

Bryson nods. "Yeah, right." He steps back and begins piling wood in the truck again. "We should probably get back soon."

I hop down. "Here, I'll help."

We grab a few more pieces of wood, then Bryson shuts the tailgate with a firm slam. "Carleigh, do you think – I don't know about you, but Quinn's been on my ass about you for a long time now, and I'd rather not give him the satisfaction 'til we've worked out, um – like, worked out what this –"

He looks so helpless and nervous, so I cut him off, taking pity. I know exactly what he means. "I agree," I reply, and he looks relieved. "I really like you, Bryson," I add gently. "A lot. But we live together and it's complicated and I think we should take it slow. Including maybe not making a big deal out of it yet to our friends."

Bryson taps his temple, finger brushing against his backward baseball cap. "Same page, Carleigh." He opens the door of the truck for me, then goes around to the driver's side and gets in himself. When we're inside, he adds, "To be clear, if they ask, I don't want to lie."

"No, of course not," I say quickly. "But no – like, no announcements."

He nods and starts the truck. I watch him stare at the steering wheel for a second. Then he undoes his seat belt, leans over, and kisses me. His palm rests on my thigh gingerly.

The kiss is short and chaste, but it takes all of my willpower not to part my legs and drag his hand between them. When he pulls back, he's smiling. "I'm real happy, Carleigh. What a great weekend."

∼

REMARKABLY, the weekend gets better after that. We don't have a chance to be alone again, but - maybe I love camping after all? Everything seems calmer here, lighter; the air is cleaner, the sun is warmer, and I can breathe. Maybe Bryson's onto something.

Bishop and Bryson build a fire, and they make steaks in the cast iron pan for dinner with some easy Caesar salad that Quinn and I made. Molly and Sawyer take care of the few dishes afterward, and as the sun starts to move lower in the sky, we all gravitate closer to the fire.

Bryson's face glows like an oil painting with the refracted light from the fire. He's laughing at something Sawyer said, his eyes bright and his grin wide, and all I can do is just look at him and wonder what the hell somebody as happy and full of life and genuinely nice could want with someone like me? If I hadn't been living with him for months now I would think that he was too good to be true. I've never met anyone quite like him in my life.

I make a s'more when the ingredients are dragged out. "If I'd have known, I'd have made homemade marshmallows to bring."

"Oh man, you haven't lived 'til you've had a s'more with Carleigh's marshmallows," Molly says enthusiastically. "You truly haven't."

"Now you tell us!" Bishop complains.

"I'll definitely bring them next time," I promise. I slide my roasted marshmallow between the graham crackers, next to the chocolate. "It's definitely been a long time since I've had one of these. Probably a year."

"Stick with us, bud!" Bryson proclaims. "We like to head out to the woods a lot. Get all the s'mores in."

"Hmm." I smile at him; I can't help it. "Did you guys have these last night?"

Quinn shakes his head. "No, we didn't get here until around supper, then we had to set up everything and eat, and Bryson made us all go to bed early so we could be awake to see you before your race started."

"Oh." I blush and stare at the fire, suddenly glad for its hypnotic dance - no one will be looking at me. "Well, I really

- thank you guys so much for coming. It means a lot to me." And it does; with the exception of Bryson and Molly, these are people that I've only even met a few times. Sure, there's the overlapping benefit of a camping trip, but even if it'd started with that, they'd chosen an entire destination specifically because of me. I've never felt so loved.

Later, Sawyer asks, "Anyone got any new ghost stories?"

"No," Bryson begins, "but there are two people here who haven't heard the Rat King story!"

I wince. "Rat King?"

Bishop reaches over and touches my arm. "It's a great story."

"Always worth hearing again," Delaney agrees, stretching his feet out. They get a little close to the fire, and his ankle gets hit with a small ember. "Ouch!" he exclaims, rubbing it. "Hey guys, the fire is hot."

Bryson grins at him. "Good tip, bud!"

I just shake my head, then tug my knees into my chest and settle in while Bryson starts telling about a construction job he once had that happened to be at a Dunkin Donuts location. Bryson's not that great at telling stories, generally speaking - that much I could've guessed - so he meanders off into tangents for a little while until finally revealing the disgusting climax of the tale, which is about a petrified dead rat they found underneath a pile of stale doughnuts.

I'm glad I didn't hear this story when I was still in my homemade doughnuts phase. That alone would've gotten me to switch to croissants.

"That's absolutely vile," Molly marvels, laughing. "I can't believe that. I'll never have Dunkin Donuts again."

"I'm sure there aren't rats in every location," Bryson

hedges. "But the food's not that great so you're not missing much."

"Oh, you take that back," Quinn says warningly.

"No, I stand by it," Bryson proclaims. "You want to fight?"

I roll my eyes. "Oh my god, every time with you two." I turn to Bishop. "What's wrong with them?"

17
CARLEIGH

I sleep like a log.

It's incredible. I'm usually a pretty poor sleeper. Changing that is on my list of self-care goals to accomplish - most of which are unchecked, save for 'run a marathon' now - but until I find the magic elixir to sleeping well, I've learned to deal with it. More or less, anyway. But not last night – I'm not sure if it's the twenty-six miles I ran or the fresh air all day or some combination of the two, but I went to bed earlier than everyone else after nearly falling asleep by the fire, and basically collapsed into the sleeping bag Molly lent me. I hadn't even been bothered by the sounds of the rest of my friends talking by the fire into the night; as soon as my head hit the pillow, I was out.

But this morning, I need to pee. Really badly. And brush my teeth - I skipped it last night, accidentally, and my mouth feels vile.

It's fairly early still, and it seems like nobody else is awake when I step out of the tent with my toothbrush and contacts case. I trudge down to the bathrooms, use the facilities, and head back when I see a tall, familiar figure just ahead of me on the path.

"Bryson?" I whisper, not wanting to wake anyone up around us.

The figure turns; it is indeed Bryson. "Carleigh!" he says happily. "What are you doing up?"

"Shh," I say, pointing to the nearest occupied campsite, which is one over from ours. "Don't want to wake them."

"They went fishing early this morning already," Bryson says. "I saw 'em go."

"Oh." I hold up my little overnight case. "Had to use the bathroom, figured I'd brush my teeth and put my contacts in while I was at it."

"Same." He points to the toothbrush holder sticking out of his shorts pocket. "Well, I've been up for a while, actually. You know me, I'm an early riser. But especially when we're camping. You start hearing the noises, the birds, and the air's cold, and yeah. Makes you get up, ya know?"

I nod, step forward, and slip my arms around his waist. "Yeah, I know," I whisper, rising on my toes to kiss him.

"Mm." He smiles into the kiss, running his hands along my back. "I'm never going to get used to this."

"Get used to what?" I ask, touching my lips to his in between each word.

Bryson breaks the kiss and pulls back to look at me. "Kissing you." His hands rub the sides of my hips, feeling the soft material of my flannel pajama bottoms. "I love the flannel, but I have to say I'm kind of partial to your little doughnut shorts."

I giggle and lean into him, suddenly grateful for the early

wake up. Without it, we wouldn't have the privacy for this, for him to smile at me so specifically with a cheeky glint in his eye as he slips his hands down and grabs my ass affectionately. "I wonder why."

"You know why, babe," Bryson laughs. He ducks his head down to kiss me one more time. "You're so pretty," he says against my lips, as softly as I've ever heard him speak. "Like this, first thing in the morning, And any time after that."

I blush and press my face into his chest. "Thanks, Bryson." I breathe him in again, taking the time to savor the moment. "We should probably get back."

He takes my hand. It's the first time he's held it since I kissed him yesterday, and I'm happy to report it still makes my stomach flip. I try to memorize how it feels; his palm big is warm and rough around mine. As I make a mental note of how small my hand is compared to his, I wonder how other things will fit.

Mind out of the gutter.

"Please tell me you brought coffee," I say as we walk up to the campsite, hands dropping.

Bryson laughs as he lifts a cooler out of the back of the truck. "Obviously, Carleigh. I don't have a death wish."

It's like Molly wants me to have completely unbridled anxiety today.

Logically, I know it wouldn't have mattered. Molly could've packed me black high-necked one-piece instead and I would still have been nervous to wear a bathing suit in front of Bryson, even now. But because she didn't, because she instead chose to saddle me with a striped turquoise-and-white bikini, I become extra anxious.

It's going to be fine, probably. That's what my rational

brain is telling me. Running has toned my body a bit and I've lost a little weight since buying the suit to begin with, so it fits pretty great. The color isn't awful and doesn't make my pale skin look alien like so many things can. Plus, it has a pretty full-coverage bottom and a decently supportive top with an actual underwire. Really, I have underwear that are a lot worse than this.

The beach we end up going to is a short drive away and is next to a hike that we might do later - not Bryson, since his ankle isn't completely healed yet - so Bishop's car is packed with changes of clothes and towels, plus six people. Me, Molly, Sawyer, and Bishop himself squeeze into the backseat, since nobody can fathom making either Bryson or Quinn do it. When we get to the beach, Molly, Sawyer, and I stake out a good spot and begin setting our stuff up.

The guys dump the towels in a pile next to them, peel their shirts off, and immediately make a break for the water. I'm grateful for the cover that my sunglasses provide; I'm not sure I can stop myself from looking at Bryson. We live together and I'm sort of a new-age hippie in many respects, so really, I've seen him shirtless before - but it feels different now that I could, theoretically, go run my hands across his chest, now that all of that muscle may be used for my benefit one day soon.

"Animals," Sawyer scoffs, peeling off the casual dress she's wearing and laying down on a towel. Molly follows suit, grabbing a magazine, so I have no choice but to fall in line. I take my shorts and tank top off and lay down on my beach towel, propping myself up with my hands so I can watch the guys be lunatics in the water.

"How long have you known them, Sawyer?" Molly asks.

"Long time," Sawyer answers. "Like fourth grade, after I moved to New Jersey from Dallas."

"Have they always been crazy?" I joke.

Sawyer nods seriously. "Yeah. Bishop's a bit more level-headed than Quinn or Bryson - my theory is because he's also got immigrant parents. Bit stricter. Plus the whole coming-out thing; he's had more time for self-reflection. But Bryson and Quinn have always been off the wall. Especially, Bryson. Some days I still think he was raised by wolves."

"That'd explain a lot."

Sawyer pulls a book out of her beach bag and opens it to a bookmarked page. Without looking at me, she says, "You know he's into you, right?"

I blush and look down. "Er -"

"I get that it's weird that you're roommates, but if it's mutual, for what it's worth I always thought he'd make a great boyfriend. He's one-hundred percent not my type," Sawyer emphasizes, glancing up, "but he's always treated his girlfriend really well."

"That's good to know, right Carleigh?" Molly says pointedly, elbowing me.

I glare at her. "Sure." I look away, chewing on my bottom lip, and wish I brought headphones so I could ignore Molly.

"Holy shit," Molly gasps, grabbing my arm. "Something happened, didn't it?"

Sawyer sets her book down. "Wait, is something actually going on between you two?"

I hesitate. We decided not to tell anyone right away before we could actually figure it out ourselves, but we also agreed not to lie, so I feel stuck. "Er. I - um -"

"Out with it, Murphy," Molly orders.

I sigh and turn to the side, away from the water, so I can speak quietly to Molly and Sawyer. "You can't say anything," I start, making sure to take my sunglasses off and make eye contact, so they know I'm serious. "But I kissed him."

"What?" Molly shrieks.

"Shut up!" I hiss, looking over my shoulder. The guys are still in the water, far enough away, but still I turn back. "Shh."

Molly winces. "Sorry. But what?" she half-whispers. "You kissed? When?"

"Yesterday," I admit. "When we get to get wood. He was being really sweet, and it just kind of ... happened."

"This is adorable," Sawyer declares, a wide grin on her face. "He's so into you, Carleigh. I've known him a long time and I've never seen him this far gone."

I duck my head again and my face feels warm. "Yeah?"

"Absolutely."

"Wait, so are you guys together now?" Molly asks, her hands clasped together conspiratorially.

"I don't really know," I answer honestly. "We haven't time to talk about it. We agreed we wouldn't say anything unless somebody directly asked, so that we can give ourselves some space to figure it out." I draw my bottom lip into my mouth and worry it between my teeth. "It's kind of complicated. He's my roommate and that works really well, and I don't want that to be screwed up, but there's also been kind of a ... thing, I guess you could say, between us for a while now and I can't ignore it any longer." I swallow a lump in my throat, feeling my anxiety rise in my chest, and pick at my toenail polish nervously. "Please don't say anything to anyone."

"Aw, Carleigh," Molly says sympathetically. "We won't."

"Vow of silence," Sawyer agrees.

Molly rubs my back. "This is really good. I know your jar is usually half-empty, but trust me. This is really good."

I nod, trying to let her words sink in. I believe them. I do.

"Don't look now, but lover boy is headed this way," Molly whispers.

I immediately clear my throat and try to look normal. I slip my sunglasses back on and stretch my legs out, making a little face to myself at how incredibly pale they look compared to the bright pink of the towel.

Bryson's shadow reaches me before he does. "Hello ladies," he says with a big smile, dripping water onto Molly's feet. "How are things up here?" He squints at me and pushes his unruly curls back from his forehead.

"Well, we were getting a good tan until a giant blocked our sun," Sawyer informs him. "You get a good wrestling match in with your boyfriends out there?"

"Ha!" Bryson chuckles. He sticks his thumb over his shoulder, toward the lake. "Either one of those bozos would be lucky to have me!"

I laugh. "We're doing fine up here, Bryson."

He squats down next to me, all long limbs and tanned skin. "You sure?" he asks, the corner of his mouth tugging upward. "You don't want to come for a dip?"

"I'm good here," I reply, turning to look for my book in her beach bag. "We're just - eek!" I squeal, as I'm suddenly lifted into the air. The world is a blur for a second, and when I'm righted again I find myself bent over Bryson's shoulder. "Bryson, you put me down right now!"

"No can do, Carleigh," he says cheerfully, as he begins walking toward the water. I look helplessly at Molly and

Sawyer, who are laughing as they get smaller in my field of vision. "I think you need a little swim."

"Bye, Carleigh!" Molly calls, waving.

"I hate you both!" I holler back. I swat at Bryson's back and cling onto his shoulders, not wanting to be put upside down. "Bryson, don't you dare put me into that water."

I can hear Bishop and Quinn laughing now. I manage to glimpse behind me just as Bryson starts wading into the lake. I steel myself to be dropped into the cold water, but he doesn't set me down yet. Instead, he keeps walking further out, past a cackling Bishop and Quinn, until my dangling feet are wet.

"Carleigh, you can swim, right?" Bryson asks.

"Yes, but don't you dare-"

He tosses me then, up and out, and I land with a splash. It's deep enough here that I can't touch but Bryson and Quinn probably can. I'm underwater for a second, where it's all swirling murky coldness, but I'm a great swimmer - earned through years at the Cape - and I surface without issue.

Bryson is nearby, standing in chin-deep water, laughing.

"I'm going to get you!" I holler, and begin to swim toward him.

"Counting on it, babe," he says, when I get to him. He reaches out for me, but I evade his grasp and swim around to his back. I push my feet at his hips, drawing myself upward and out of the water, then sits on his shoulders and dunk his head underwater.

Bryson bucks me off easily, which I assumed, but even though I'm tossed in the water again it's still worth it to see him sputtering and wet like a retriever when his head surfaces again.

"You got me, Carleigh," he crows happily. "We're even!"

"Mm. We'll see." I swim closer to him and paddle myself in a slowly narrowing circle until his guard lowers. Then I kick backward, splashing a broad spray of water in his face.

"Oh god!" he exclaims, turning to shield himself. "Uncle, uncle!"

I laugh and stop kicking. I've got a good front crawl and I'm back at his side quickly. "Truce?" I ask, treading water in front of him.

Bryson sweeps his hair back again. "Truce," he agrees. "Come here."

I glance over at Bishop and Quinn. They've somehow found a beach ball - they definitely hadn't brought one with them, so I'm not sure how that happened - and are tossing it back and forth where the water is shallower. I can also see Sawyer and Molly still on the beach, both with reading material - though if I know my best friend, I'm sure Molly is actually watching us.

But Molly knows now, so I figure it's safe enough. I swim to him and slips my legs around his waist. The water is buoyant enough for me just to loosely hang onto his shoulders, but he still supports me with an arm around my hips.

"Hi," I say.

"Hey, Carleigh." Bryson's smile is almost warm enough to soothe the sting of the cool lake water.

I let one of my hands fall under the surface. I slide my palm onto Bryson's chest, the way I've been imagining since earlier, and give him a sly smile. "It's a good thing I had sunglasses on earlier," I say softly. "Couldn't stop staring at you when you took your clothes off. Wish I could kiss you."

A muscle twitches in Bryson's jaw. "Speak for yourself, babe," he whispers. He brings a hand to my waist under the water and drags his knuckles across my stomach. "There's lots of things I want to do to you in this thing." His index finger traces the cup of my bikini top. His eyes are watching my face intently.

My breath catches. "Bryson."

"They aren't looking, Carleigh," he says, but he doesn't go in for a kiss. He does palm at my breast carefully, watching me the whole time.

My eyelids flutter closed. God. Even here, with the barrier of water and the fabric of my suit between us, his hands are incredible. I want so much more. But we're in a lake with our friends. So - "We should stop," I say, unwinding my legs from him.

Bryson nods and drops his hands obediently. I swing myself around to his back and slip on, hanging my arms around his neck and my chin over his shoulder. "To higher ground!"

"You're um - you're going to have to give me a sec," he mutters. His hands tighten around the back of my knees.

Oh. I bite my lower lip and wait patiently. I rest my cheek on his shoulder, not caring at this point, and look out at the lake. It really is beautiful; I just might get used to this.

18
CARLEIGH

The night goes late.

The group stops being loud around eleven, in accordance with the campground rules, but our fire burns until after one in the morning. But even then, after the full day of sun and water and that evening's impromptu beer darts tournament, I can't sleep. Maybe the fresh air thing is a lie after all..

I stare at the roof of the tent I'm sharing with Sawyer and Molly, thinking about Bryson. How is any of this supposed to work? It's too new of a relationship - if it even is that - for us to actually live together, like same-bedroom-same-closet live together. At the same time, it seems odd for us to keep living like nothing's changed. And yet still, I don't want him to move out.

I've accounted for none of this in my five-year plan.

"Carleigh, I can hear you thinking," Molly mumbles sleepily. "Everything okay?"

I turn over in my sleeping bag. "Yeah. Just trying to work something out."

Molly lifts herself up on her elbow. "Why don't you go over to Bryson's tent and let him work it out?" she teases in a light whisper. Even in the darkness, I can see her devilish grin.

"Oh." I flop onto my pillow. "It's not that."

"Well, whatever it is, maybe you just need to talk to him."

I close my eyes for a moment, listening to the dying crackle of the campfire. It's mostly out now; I can smell the smoke. "It's the middle of the night."

"Go on, Carleigh," Sawyer pipes in softly. "He's got his own tent. Go for a walk or something."

"No, I ..." I trail off, confused again. It feels rude to go wake Bryson up, but on the other hand, we really need to think through the logistics of this whole thing. I do some of my best work late at night; why would this be any different?

So, I unzip my sleeping bag and quietly put my flip-flops on.

"Go to sleep," I tell my friends, then silently slip out of the tent.

I make my way as quietly as possible over to the small one-man tent that I know belongs to Bryson. It's dark inside, but I don't hear the faint snoring that I occasionally hear from his bedroom, so he must be at least mostly awake. I slowly undo the zipper of the tent and kneel just inside.

Gently, I shake his leg. "Bryson," I whisper.

He stirs, slightly at first, then sits up in a panic when he realizes who it is. "Carleigh?" he says. "Everything okay?"

"Shh," I hush, putting a finger in front of my lips. "I wanted ... do you want to go for a walk?"

It's dark, but the moonlight streaming in behind me has illuminated his face enough for me to see the soft look on his face. "Yeah," he whispers. "Okay, yeah."

I wait for him on the road between campsites while he gets dressed. It doesn't take long. As soon as he reaches me, he takes my hand. We don't talk for nearly five minutes as we walk among silent tents and campers; it's only when we're far enough away from people and have reached the concrete slip of the boat launch and accompanying docks that he speaks.

"I hope this isn't you dragging me out of bed to break up with me before we're even dating," Bryson says, honest like always.

I'm alarmed by that. "What? No, of course not," I assure him, giving him a quick peck on the lips before we walk down to sit at the end of the dock.

Bryson folds himself down onto the wood. "Okay, so what are you messing up my beauty sleep for?"

I sit down next to him, cross legged, and shrug somewhat miserably. "I couldn't sleep," I confess. "I just kept thinking about how it'll work at home, and that it's too soon to move into one bedroom, but is it weird to have a first date with someone you share a bathroom with? How do I get dressed up if you're there watching me?"

To my surprise, Bryson just gives me a soft smile. "Carleigh."

"What?"

He chuckles. "That brain of yours is really working overtime all the time, isn't it?" He moves his legs around to bracket me, pulling me to sit facing him, between his legs, so I can see his face. My knees fall in line with his hips. "Carleigh, I'll do whatever it takes to work. I'll leave while you're getting dolled up. You don't have to get dolled up, but if you want to, I'll leave. I'll go get cheap flowers and knock on the door and the whole nine yards, if it helps." He strokes my waist. "It's a little unconventional, but I like that, baby. And I like you. And that's all that matters. The rest of that is all just noise. Okay?"

I smile at him, already feeling less stressed out. He always seems to know what to say and how to say it. He's definitely on the sensitive side, as far as emotional intelligence goes. I wonder if he's this in tune with everybody, or if it's just me.

"Okay," I agree, leaning in for a kiss.

Bryson returns it, slow and languid, like we should be waking up instead of going to sleep. He sweeps my hair off my shoulders, then slides his hands under my ass and lifts me into his lap. I giggle softly into his mouth and curl my legs around his waist, tugging myself closer.

I love making out with Bryson, I've officially decided. He's good at it, first of all - how could he not be a great kisser, a man who loves running his mouth as much as he does? - and he always knows just where to skim his fingertips, just how to hold me. I can't wait to discover all of the other things he's probably good at. Not here, of course – I want him, but I'm not that much a slave to my basic desires that I'm going to have sex with him on a cold wooden dock in the middle of the Adirondacks.

Not for the first time, anyway.

I'm not opposed to doing a little more, though, so I grip his wrist and intentionally move his hand from my hips to beneath my shirt. I've been trying to sleep, so I'm not wearing a bra; Bryson kisses me harder as the realization of it dawns on him, swallowing the moan I let out as he palms my breasts.

"So goddamn beautiful, Carleigh," he tells me between messy kisses, as he slips his other hand beneath my shirt as well. "Every part of you." He cups both of my breasts, squeezing firmly.

Bryson's touch is tender and impolite at the same time. His big hands move both gently and roughly; he tugs at my nipples and then pinches them lightly in unison. That move elicits a delighted gasp from me, I rolls my hips against him and bites his earlobe.

"I need you," I exhale, leaning back a little. He moves one hand to my back to support me and intuitively moves the other near my stomach. "Please, Bryson," I whine. "I need you."

Bryson slides his hand beneath the waistband of my pajama pants and cups me between my legs, over my underwear. "Jesus, baby," he mutters, fingertips pressing over my entrance. "You're so wet. You're going to ruin your pajamas."

I swallow and lean my head back to look at the stars, not caring anymore. I don't care, he should tear my underwear off, I just want - "Want you to ruin me," I breathe, before realizing I said it out loud.

Bryson goes still. "Carleigh," he finally says, ragged. "You can't - if you want slow, baby, you can't say stuff like that."

Slow.

Right.

I breathe deeply, in and out, practicing my pranayama. "This probably isn't slow, huh?" I ask, once I can speak again. The tight coil in my abdomen is beginning to unwind.

Bryson's hand slides out of my bottoms and returns to my waist. He tugs me into him, hugging me tightly.

"I wasn't lying today, Carleigh," he mutters quietly. "I'm going to be honest: there's a lot I want to do with you, a lot I've thought about. Some of it's not even dirty stuff! And so far, everything's been a lot better than I imagined. But I'm going to take you apart, Carleigh. Piece by piece. That's a promise." His grip tightens on my waist. "But not here. You deserve better than that."

I nod into his neck and press a soft kiss to his pulse point. "I look forward to it," I whisper.

We sit for a while longer and then head back to the campsite, hand-in-hand again. I follow Bryson into his tent. He tucks me into his arms, drags the unzipped sleeping bag over us on his single air mattress like a blanket, and kisses me softly.

"Night, babe," he whispers.

I burrow into his chest and shut my eyes. "Night," I echo.

19

BRYSON

I'm the luckiest son of a bitch in the world.

It's mid-afternoon on a Wednesday, but it's raining so work ends early. I take the train home happily, not even caring that I am drenched because I forgot to bring an umbrella. I stop on the way to the apartment to buy a small bouquet of tulips from a nearly rained-out vendor; there's not that many people out given the weather and the time of day, but I see this guy all the time here selling flowers and I've got a soft spot for him. Besides, now I've got someone to give them to.

Carleigh.

I'm not foolish enough to think she's the only reason I'm happy today. I'm an upbeat guy for the most part. What's not to like? My life is going pretty great: I have a job I don't hate, my friends and family are healthy, I live in a great city.

But obviously, there's been a shift in my relationship with Carleigh, and the impact of this has been indescribable. I know I've always kind of had my head in the clouds. But now that Carleigh and I are a real Carleigh-and-me, I'm basically living my life on the moon.

I let myself into the apartment and can see by a pair of still-drying flats by the door that Carleigh's home, too. That fact prompts a smile. "Honey!" I call out, channeling my inner Fred Flintstone. "I'm home!"

Carleigh pops her head around the corner. "Hey, you're home early!" she remarks. She's in the kitchen, like usual, but she drops her spatula to come greet me. She stops short of a hug and exclaims, "Oh Bryson, you're soaked!"

I look at her innocently. "I maybe didn't look at the forecast before I left for work this morning. But here!" I thrust the tulips at her.

She smiles at the flowers, takes them, and sets them in the kitchen. "Bryson, you're too much."

"People have been saying that my whole life, babe." I unlace my work boots and slip them off. "Now come, give me a hug." I open my arms but she declines, pointing at the puddle that's following me. I shrug and gather her up in my arms anyway, chuckling as she squeals and pushes at me.

"Bryson," she whines. "These are clean clothes."

That makes me laugh. "Your finest sweatpants," I tease, tilting her head up to kiss her. She tastes like chocolate chips; clearly, it's going to be a good night.

"Don't mock my sweatpants." Carleigh gives me a cross look, but she squeezes my biceps, so I know she's not actually mad. I flex them, winking at her.

I've noticed over the past two weeks we've been more-than-friends that Carleigh's got a bit of a thing for my arms. I'm not complaining; I've spent a lot of hours hauling heavy things around, and occasionally lifting weights with Bishop, and it's nice to have someone appreciate it.

I decide to take advantage of this fact by peeling off my soaked t-shirt. Carleigh bites her bottom lip as her eyes fall across my chest. "Oh come on, Bryson, now you've got me all confused."

"What?" I exclaim, laughing. I step away from her and turn the light to the oven on so I can see what she's baking. "What do you mean?"

"I mean, you're dripping water all over the floor so I want you to go change, but now I also want to make out."

"Ah. The eternal dilemma." I wink at her, flip the oven light off, and stamps a kiss on her mouth. "Luckily, we can have both. Come on."

Carleigh looks between me and the timer on the oven. "My cookies will be done in two minutes," she says. "Go change and I'll come as soon as I can take them out."

I flash her a faux-offended look. "Wow, Carleigh," I say, shaking my head. "Glad to see where your priorities are."

She nods at me, looking serious. "Yes, Bryson. Always cookies first."

I laugh and go to my bedroom, picking up my wet t-shirt along the way. I discard both it and the soaked pants in the laundry, then pull a clean pair of jeans and one of my oldest t-shirts on. I plop my ball cap on top of my dresser to dry out and make a half-hearted attempt to fix my hair before I give up and lay on the bed.

It still feels a little odd to be here, waiting for my gorgeous, too-good-for-me roommate to come in so we can make out. I can't believe that out of all of the guys in New York, I'm the lucky asshole that's with Carleigh. It's only been two weeks since she'd kissed me in Lake Placid, but we're definitely among the better two weeks of my life. Until now, I don't think that I've been truly aware of how much of my energy had been taken up by thinking about Carleigh, worrying about Carleigh, and dreaming about Carleigh. I still do, but now that we're together, in whatever manner of speaking, there's an underlying certainty to it all that's helped me relax about it all.

Carleigh comes in after a few minutes. Her casual style hasn't changed since the shift between us- she still spends most of her time in loose dresses, sweatpants, jeans, and t-shirts - but now that I've got more of an idea of what's underneath it all, I have really come to appreciate it a lot more. I love her sweatpants, the way they fit her round ass, how they cuff at her ankles, and how it's so easy to slip my hand inside of them. I like her shirts, too; there's always been a delicious stretch across her chest, but now I'm intimately familiar with the soft, sensitive skin beneath, the sharp point of her waist, her curvy hips. And she's so unassuming about it all, sometimes still so shy when I take her shirt off. I can't understand how she doesn't realize what she does to me.

Today, though, she seems a little more confident. I like when she's in this mood, when her chin is high and her chest is proud. Carleigh climbs onto the bed, bites her lip, and straddles me. I don't say anything, don't move, just watches her with a smile as she appraises me.

"You put a shirt on," she observes.

"You told me to go change!"

Carleigh leans forward slightly, her hips tilting against mine, and runs her hands up my abdomen to my shoulder. "You could've left that off."

I lean up to meet her and catch her mouth in a kiss. "I'll remember that for next time," I murmured against her lips, my fingers weaving into her loose braid. I trail my other hand up her back delicately, then press my knuckles against the spot where I know she always develops stress knots.

Carleigh groans at the sensation and breaks the kiss, dropping her face into my neck. "Bryson, holy hell," she breathes. "God, I love your hands."

I laugh softly at that. She's told me before, but I'll never tire of hearing the things she loves about me. She loves my arms, loves my hands, loves how strong I am. My eyes are pretty, I've got a nice ass, my ADD stresses her out but it's endearing, too. I want to hear it all, all the time.

I slide a hand down and grip her ass, squeezing it as I tug her against me. "Love touching you," I tell her, and it's true. I love her perfect little body under my hands, from her soft stomach to her smooth legs to her pale neck. I love the way her breasts just spill out of my large palms, how her hips sometimes buck when I grope at her ass, and how warm she is around my fingers when my hand moves inside her underwear.

The last one is fairly new. Carleigh and I agreed to take it slow, and aside from a handful of times when we have almost thrown that out the window, we've tried to stick to it. It's been difficult: I live with the girl I'm pretty sure I'm in love with, and she's funny and sexy and around all the time. I've always been more of a throw-caution-to-the-wind type of guy, always leaped in with both feet before looking. It's just who I am. But Carleigh's a planner, a thinker. She likes to analyze before reaching a point of no return.

Which is kind of foolish, because I'm almost certain we

reached that point two months after moving into her apartment.

She wants me, though. She's said it to me plainly, but I could tell before that, from the first time we kissed by a woodpile somewhere upstate. It was there in the way she moved her leg around me, and the next night, when I first touched her by the lake. When she's ready, really ready - not a request in the throes of passion, but when I can tell in her eyes that she won't regret anything - I can't wait to be inside her.

Not that we've done nothing. I'm not a saint and I know Carleigh isn't either. She's come apart around my hand twice now, and two days ago, she'd slid onto her knees in the living room between my thighs. It's a matter of time. I'm leaving her promises every day and soon, I know she'll collect.

"Mm." Carleigh's hands blindly push around my waist, until finally they grip the hem of my shirt and she tugs at it. "Off," she requests.

I obey, quickly sitting up and reaching behind myself to gather a handful of fabric in my palm. I pull my shirt over my head and then grip her hips, flipping us easily so Carleigh is now flat on her back. She squeals in surprise but looks up at me after, her already-dark eyes impossibly more so, and touches my arms again. She wraps one of her legs around me and pulls me down on top of her.

I don't let my full weight fall on her, obviously; I half-hover over her, propped on one elbow, and kisses her. "You're full of surprises, Carleigh," I mutter, dragging my mouth to her neck.

She tilts her head backward to give me better access. "How so?"

I push her shirt up as I suck a bruise onto her pulse point. I soothe it with my tongue, then slide a hand under her back to unhook her bra. "You're little miss in-charge," I say, as I pull her upper back upward rather unceremoniously so I can tug off her shirt and slide the bra off of her arms. "You like being bossy. But you love me throwing you around."

I shift a little lower on the bed when I lay her back down, then draws her nipple into my mouth. I circle my tongue and then bites down lightly; she grabs a handful of my hair, and I releases her nipple, grinning.

Her cheeks are reddened when I glance up. *Shit.* I decide the only way out is through.

I fondle the breast I just lavished and turn my mouth to the other one. "It's okay, babe," I say. "Don't be shy. I love doing it."

Carleigh whines a little and cants her hips upward. "Yeah?"

I squeeze her breasts roughly, watching her gasp a little and then look down at me with heavily lidded eyes. "Yeah," I repeat, doing it again. I never want to hurt her, and she obviously loves what I'm doing right now, but I also be lying if I said hurting her in general wasn't one of my concerns. I've had this problem before: I'm a big guy, and she's so much smaller than me.

I release her breasts and watch a brief redness bloom over her pale skin. Then I roll off her and shift back upward along the bed. I'm not done with her, though; as soon as I can reach, I kiss her soundly, then push at her sweatpants with my right hand.

Carleigh lifts her hips immediately. "Take them off," she breathes.

I do, tugging them to her ankles and then letting her kick them off the rest of the way. She bends her knees toward herself and I catch one of them, run my hand up her calf and massage her thigh before I pull her knee down to part her legs.

She's got underwear on, but she's so wet that it may as well not matter. Her chest is moving rapidly with her breath, but I'm cautious of her comfort and don't yank off her panties like I'd really like to. Instead, I cup her between her legs, letting her adjust, then slip my hand underneath them.

She feels like Christmas morning, or something equally cheesy. I kiss her through the slow inhale that she gives as I slip one finger inside her. "Okay?" I ask.

Carleigh nods, eyes closed, and adjusts her hips a bit. "Another," she requests, ears turning pink. "Please, Bryson-"

I add a second finger, my eyes fixed on the delighted wince on her face. I haven't been around the block or anything, but I've had my share of girlfriends, and my big hands have usually served me well in this department. I slide my thumb to move in small circles on her clit, coaxing her deeper, and crook my fingers slightly as I begin to move them inside of her.

"Fuck," she breathes, her eyes screwed shut. "Don't stop, Bryson."

Not for the world, not with her almost naked on my hand, not with that furrowed, concentrated look on her face. Never. "I won't, babe," I promise. I'm still propped on one elbow, but I manage to shift my arm enough to cup her right breast. I roll it in my hand, remembering the nights I dreamed of a moment like this, and drop my mouth to her nipple at the same time as I increase the pressure from my thumb.

"Bryson, Bryson, Bryson," Carleigh's chanting, my name mostly air. "Bryson, Bryson, please -"

"Come on, babe," I encourage, my lips pulling at her skin. I bring my index finger to work against my thumb and wince at the hard pull she gives my hair.

A few moments later, she comes, her walls fluttering around me and her chest heaving. I kiss her as soon as she's caught her breath, rubbing her cheek with my clean hand. "So pretty, Carleigh," I say into her ear. "Fucking incredible."

"Bryson." Carleigh's eyes open lazily. She smiles, wide and slow. "You're - god, Bryson, I -"

"One sec, babe," I tell her, pecking her lips. I scramble off the bed and go to the bathroom to grab a washcloth to clean her up a bit. I'm so hard I might explode, so I slip my jeans from my hips and jerk off quickly while I'm in here. It doesn't take long; she barely touched me, but watching her fall apart like that, knowing I'm the one who made her let go - it'd been more than enough.

I go to her bedroom and grab her a clean pair of underwear, then bring them and a cloth to my room, where she's still laying on the bed. She seems a bit more awake now, the haze having lifted, and she takes both items from me when I return.

"Thanks," Carleigh says, standing. She slips her underwear off and runs the cloth between her legs and around her thighs, then puts her clean panties on. She looks a little embarrassed when she's done and stammers, "Er. Hang on."

Carleigh leaves the room with the cloth and her ruined

underwear, presumably to put them in the laundry. I pull my shirt on and am sitting on the edge of the bed when she walks back in, wearing nothing but the underwear I brought her.

I can't stop myself from letting out a swear. "Christ, Carleigh," I say, my eyes tracing her body from her feet, up her shapely legs and hips, to her perfect breasts and that beautiful face. "You look like I dreamed you up."

She blushes. "Thanks," she says, stepping toward me. Her clothes are strewn haphazardly across the bed, but instead of reaching for them, she sits down in my lap, cuddling into me.

I hold her immediately, wrapping my arm around her. "So perfect, Carleigh." I tease her nipple with my thumb. "Loved every minute."

Carleigh bites her bottom lip and drops a hand to my waistband. "What about you?" she asks softly. "Can I-"

"I, um, took care of it," I confess. "You were laying there all blissed-out - you needed that. Didn't take much," I add with a laugh.

She looks vaguely disappointed. "Next time let me," she requests, her arm around my shoulder. "Please?"

I nod and kiss her. "Alright, Carleigh."

She seems satisfied with that. She reaches behind me, straining to grab her bra and t-shirt. I help her climb over me so she's closer, but I briefly pin her to the mattress, facing down, and grip her ass with both hands.

"Love your ass," I remind her, smacking it playfully. She giggles and squirms beneath me. Taking pity, I roll away from her and successfully dodge her attempted return hit to my arm. I leave her alone while she gets dressed again, then ask, "Think the cookies are cool enough to eat yet?"

Ten minutes later, we're on the couch underneath a blanket. Rain is lashing against the windows and the forecast says a thunderstorm might be brewing, but I don't care: I've got freshly baked cookies, an unseen episode of Last Week Tonight, and Carleigh cuddled against my side.

Yeah, I'm definitely on the moon.

20

CARLEIGH

It doesn't take too long for his friends to find out about us.

This is actually fine. Molly and Sawyer managed to learn about it while we were still in Lake Placid, and while they're sworn to secrecy, I know nothing actually stays a secret forever.

Initially, we agreed not to make any announcements about our new relationship. This was at least in part because it was unclear what was specifically actually happening between us; at that point there'd been just a kiss - a great kiss, but just a kiss - and nothing about our situation loaned itself well to an obvious path forward. Accompanying that had been a let's-go-slow agreement, which both of us are probably guilty of trying to violate at various points, but at least that would inevitably have its own natural resolution. I can't wait very much longer, and know that Bryson is just waiting for my go-ahead.

Now, nearly a month in, I am certain that whatever it is

exactly between us, it's not casual, and it's not going away. Which shouldn't be a surprise; I'm a smart woman. I should've known that something between myself and Bryson could never be temporary.

We have our first official date on September first. True to his word, Bryson leaves the apartment while I get dressed. I pick a pretty green dress to go underneath my favorite jean jacket, curl my hair, and actually put on makeup. He shows up with flowers for the second time that day, since he's developed a bit of a habit of bringing me tulips from the vendor by the subway, then we go to the Court Street Grocers near Washington Square Park and spend a couple of hours just sitting by the fountain, eating sandwiches and talking.

I don't sleep with him that night, but he does give me a release on the couch when we get home, so - almost. Afterward, I tell him I want to call him my boyfriend; he gets a happy look on his face like a puppy with a treat, and god, I'm so in love.

A week after that, Quinn invites us to another opening, this time a soft launch of a new restaurant that his marketing firm is working on. He gets seats for four and manages to convince Sawyer to come along. The place is supposed to be sort of trendy, upscale-casual, but Bryson is told he has to wear a real shirt with actual buttons and a collar, and he's annoyed.

"I don't like it, Carleigh, it's itchy."

I watch him pace around the kitchen, fiddling with his cuffs. The shirt looks good on him - great, in fact. It's a nice blue color that brings out his eyes. It's not his fault that this kind of thing feels alien to him - he does seem to have been born with a fisherman's wardrobe.

"You've dressed up before, Bryson," I remind him. "You just came with me to my school thing like a month and a half ago!"

Bryson makes a face. "And it was uncomfortable then, too."

I raise an eyebrow. "You didn't say anything."

"Well, Carleigh," Bryson begins, walking over to me, "I would have, but I was busy trying to come up with excuses to hold your hand all night, and I figured you wouldn't want to if I was just complaining all night."

"But you're not worried about that now," I surmise.

Bryson places his hands on my ribcage and rubs his thumbs against the bottom curve of my breasts. "Well now you're all acquainted with the nice things I can do with my hands, Half-Sour, not as worried, no."

I laugh and push his hands to my waist. "If it helps, I was very into you that night and I'm already really into this." I rub his bicep. "And I'll hold your hand as much as you want."

"Mm, that helps a lot, Carleigh," he murmurs, dropping a kiss on my mouth. "Except Quinn and Sawyer will be there."

"Sawyer already knows," I confess, glancing sheepishly at him when he gives me an incredulous look. "She and Molly found out the day after we kissed at Lake Placid. They asked," I add hurriedly. "We said we wouldn't lie."

Bryson's jaw drops. "I can't believe you didn't tell me!"

I wince. "I didn't want - we also said we'd keep it between us for a while. I swore them both to secrecy, so that we could have time." I give him an apologetic look. "I should've told you, I'm sorry, but you said Jackson had been bothering you about it, so I didn't want you to have to tell anyone if it was going to be a problem."

"Carleigh." Bryson shakes his head at me. "Are you kidding me? Yeah then, sure - but if last week was - if what we said is happening, then I want everyone to know you're my girl. The whole freaking world! I'll rent a skywriting plane, right up there next to the clouds: 'Bryson plus Carleigh equals', then I'll get 'em to draw a squiggly little heart with the plane, though I bet that's probably pretty tricky to pull off. But that's what they're paid for, I guess! I don't know, I like to think if I was a pilot that did skywriting that I'd make sure I could do whatever the customer asked before -"

I kiss him to shut him up. He's always been a big talker, always been loud, always had lots to say.

"Anyone ever tell you that you talk too much, Bryson?" I ask, breaking the kiss.

Bryson grins. "Er, yeah, only every single teacher I ever had, plus both of my parents, and all my grandparents, and my sister..."

"Yeah, I get it," I laugh, holding a hand up to silence him. "You ready to go? We should probably go catch the train."

Bryson offers me his hand. "You got it, boss."

The subway to Lower Manhattan is fairly busy, but we're on the line early enough to get seats, which is nice. I'm not wearing a dress today instead it's my best black pants and an appropriately nice silk sleeveless top - but in an effort to be dressier I'm wearing a pair of what are not the world's comfiest flats, so sitting is welcomed. I'm short and the have high arches and I really think that one day soon I'm going to end up exclusively wearing orthopedic shoes, so I'm really trying not to push it.

Somewhere around Greenwich Village, an elderly lady with a cane gets on the train, and Bryson immediately hops up to give her his seat. "Thank you," she says, giving him a kind smile as she sits down next to me.

"No problem, ma'am!" Bryson replies cheerfully. "How's your day going?"

"Oh, it's going well," the woman answers, clearly surprised that this big burly-looking guy is talking to her. "I'm on my way to visit my sister."

"Oh really?" Bryson leans over, keeping a hand on the bar to steady himself, and continues chatting with the older woman. Her sister's mobility has been getting worse lately, so they're thinking about a nursing home, but ideally they'd like to go to the same one.

Bryson engages with this information with a characteristic balance of sensitivity and encouragement; I marvel at it. He's such a natural with people. It's jealousy-inducing. What a gift.

"Babe, which stop are we getting off at?" he asks me suddenly, glancing up at the line map.

"One more," I answer, feeling my natural shyness take over as the elderly lady glances between us.

"Oh, is this your girlfriend?" the woman asks with a warm smile. "You're very beautiful, young lady," she tells me, patting my hand.

I blush. "Oh, that's very nice of you to say, thank you."

Bryson looks at me adoringly. "She is." I press my lips together and shake my head a little at him, but don't say anything.

The woman folds her hands on her lap and smiles at us. "You're very sweet together," she says. "There's certainly nothing like young love."

"Thanks, ma'am!" Bryson says, grinning at her. "I'm going to try to keep her from coming to her senses!" The train slowly lurches to a stop and I double-check the stop before standing up. I indicate to Bryson that we should be getting off here, and he says, "Very nice meeting you, ma'am, you have a lovely day."

"Nice to meet you," I echo, and with a wave goodbye, we step onto the platform. Once we're at street level, I slip my hand into his. "So, you've never met a stranger, huh?"

Bryson shrugs. "I like yakking and old ladies like to be yakked at. Mutually beneficial, as they say."

"Hmm."

He lifts our hands to waist height. "So um - are we telling Quinn today, then?"

I grin. "I think we just let him figure it out."

We don't get the chance.

It's unplanned, but while we're waiting outside the restaurant for Sawyer and Quinn, I get an email, one that I hadn't expected for a few weeks still: an acceptance letter from the Culinary Institute of America.

I applied on a whim many months earlier, before Bryson even moved in. It isn't a realistic dream, but after splitting a bottle of wine with Trinity one night, I decided I owed it to myself to at least see if I could get into pastry school. The chances were slim, and when I didn't get in, I'd just continue on with my predetermined academia path with some kind of satisfaction that I at least entertained other avenues. It'd been a deviation in my plan, sure, but the plan allowed for thinking about other things.

It hadn't accounted for this: *a yes, Ms. Murphy, please come join us in Hyde Park for the winter session beginning in January.*

"Oh," I breathe, staring at my phone. We're leaning against the old brick of the building, waiting. My phone had buzzed with a notification from my inbox, and I decided to check just in case my professor had responded to an earlier inquiry.

Bryson, who'd been staring down the street for any sign of Sawyer or Quinn, looks over at me. "What?"

"I, um - a few months ago I applied for ... for pastry school," I stammer, still staring in disbelief at my phone. "I'd been feeling a little over it with my lit stuff, and I figured it didn't hurt to apply, probably wouldn't get in anyway but I just - Bryson, I got in." I look up at him, my brain feeling fuzzy. "I got in."

"Carleigh!" Bryson exclaims, his face immediately breaking into a grin. "That's amazing!" He sweeps me onto my toes, into a grand hug, squeezing me so tightly that I nearly can't breathe. "Why didn't you tell me you applied?" he asks, setting me down.

"I - I kind of forgot," I answer, looking at my phone again. Absurdly, I feel the burn of tears prickling at my eyes, and blink hard to stop them. "So much has happened since then, and..." I look at him again as heavy realization hits me. Hyde Park. That's too far away to commute from the city; at a minimum, I'd have to move to like, Poughkeepsie, at least for weekdays. "Bryson, it's - it's two hours away."

I'm surprised at the pit in my stomach that is beginning

to open. We've been dating for not even a month, and I've never been one to base my life decisions on any kind of personal relationship. But this thing with Bryson, it feels ... good. I don't want to ruin it, especially when it's this new. I remember how my undergrad boyfriend freaked out at me when I decided to move to Manhattan for grad school, telling me I didn't care about him or about our future - we'd been dating for barely six months, I'm not sure we had a future at that point - and so I expect Bryson's face to sour at the news.

But it doesn't. Instead, Bryson makes a who-cares face, shrugs, and pulls me into a hug again. "We'll figure it out, babe, don't worry about it." He laughs happily, presses a kiss on my hair, and gives a grand sigh. "This is the best news ever, Carleigh, I'm so proud of you. Going after what you want, doing you."

I pull back from him a bit, mostly so I can access oxygen, and nod. "You don't think it's crazy? I spent six years getting two degrees in literature, and instead, I'm going to go learn how to make kouign amann?"

"I don't know what that is, babe," Bryson says with a laugh. "Sure maybe it's a little crazy, but you seem a lot happier when you're baking than when you're doing book stuff. And life's about what makes you happy, Carleigh."

I shake my head a little at him, marveling at how simple he makes it seem. Maybe, it can be that easy.

"You make me happy," I say softly, tilting my head up.

"Back at you, babe," he answers, and kisses me.

It's not a long kiss, just a few seconds, but I get lost in him all the same. This big, burly teddy bear of a man; god, I love him, and I'd tell him right now if I didn't think it might freak him out a little, plus then I'd have to stop kissing him and I don't want that, not at all, I want to die right here attached to him, want -

"I called it!"

We break apart and turn to see Quinn standing in front of us, arms crossed, looking triumphant. He has a big, boastful grin on his face and is standing next to Sawyer, who's smiling.

"Quinn," Bryson growls playfully. "Thought you'd never show up."

"We missed the train." Quinn points between Bryson and I. "You found something to occupy your time though."

Bryson just smiles and gives a casual shrug, looping one arm around my shoulders. "She couldn't resist me any longer."

"Hmm." I roll my eyes, but can't stop myself from smiling, too. In every way, it's true.

21

CARLEIGH

I have a love-hate relationship with working at Logan's. On most days, it's love: I like my coworkers, like the regulars, like the tips. Then there are some days - blissfully few and far between, but still present - where it's more of a hate. Usually, it has something to do with an endless crowd that affords no breaks, a shitty table, or some combination of the two. Tonight is one of those nights. Pray for me.

It starts off when the bartender neglects to inform the serving staff they actually drained their last keg of a particular type of in-demand locally-brewed pilsner, and wouldn't be getting any in until the following week. I sell five pints of it before I find out, and when I go back to a table of financial bros to inform them, it didn't go so well.

"Sorry we're actually out, but have you tried the Five Mountains blonde because it's pretty similar?"

One of the men in a suit at the table, gets pissed, and

slams his fist down on the table. "Why wouldn't you tell us before we ordered? Isn't that your job?"

I scoot back a bit away from the table, and bring my pen and pad back out. "I can get you the Five Mountains blonde, or something else to replace it. They just told me," I reply.

"Why don't you bring us some of that and then come have a seat," he says, and pats his lap.

Do guys think that's sexy? I'm sure there is some girl that will fall for it, but not me. My standards are way higher than this sleazebag. The suit is custom which means it costs a pretty penny, and this guy is probably not used to hearing no.

So, instead of responding, I just walk away and let a male server take over the table. It's a gamble with a group like that. They will either leave a very generous tip or leave none at all. Usually, the more you flirt, the better the tip, but I'm not one of girls that is comfortable flirting with strangers for money.

It gets busier after that, and there's no natural break between the after-work crowd and the early-night crowd, so I don't get a chance to eat. All the stress from college is over, and I can finally catch a break.

Hyde Park isn't the same. My love for baking isn't stressful, and it's a different feel from academics. This is my chance to learn some new tricks and show off my creative side. I still can't believe they accepted me, and I leave in on Sunday. Three hours isn't that far away, but it still makes it impossible to live in Hell's Kitchen and get back and forth every day.

Right before my shift comes to an end, I wait on my last table. At this point, I'm getting hangry, and just want to get home and cook something to eat, but this table is taking their sweet time. It is two men who appear to be in the financial industry to some degree, talking about stocks, and when I go over to ask if they are ready for their check, he tries to rub the back of my thigh. Before I can think about it, my hand is going across his face. I should have let the bouncers handle it.

"What the hell is wrong with you?" the man asks, holding his face. "Let me talk to your boss."

The security guy walks over, and stands by me, while he talks to the manager. He denies trying to feel me up, and honestly it's my last shift anyway. I just want to get the hell out of here.

My boss pulls me to the back, and assures me that everything is fine. It's not like he is going to fire me. Technically, I was supposed to be off the clock almost an hour ago.

"He's talking about suing, but that's just how these type of men are. I won't hold my breath."

I grab the jacket and purse out of my locker, and head outside toward the train. Logan's has agreed to hire me back once I'm done with Hyde Park. One less thing I need to worry about when I get back. It's crucial for me to have a job, but Bryson has agreed to take care of the rent while I'm gone. Technically, I could have asked my parents, but I'm not sure how they are going to feel about me going to this school.

On the train home, I think about how things might go at Hyde Park, and if I'm cut out for this. Self-doubt is something I've always struggled with, even a girl with a background like me. Bryson might not even be home - he mentioned maybe handing out with Max- but I send him a text any way.

Me: On the way home. Had a bad shift today, didn't get to eat. Please tell me there's still chicken left over from yesterday.

Bryson's reply is almost instantaneous.

Bryson: I ate it, but I'll have something waiting for you!

I send a smile back and then put my phone away. One-thirty in the morning is such an odd time to be eating, but at this point, I would even be willing to eat a pile of raw pastry dough, just to fill my stomach.

I don't end up needing to. When I step into the apartment, I'm hit with the smell of buttery pasta. Bryson's at the stove, mixing the last of a pile of grated cheese into a pot.

"Mac and cheese," I breathe, kicking my shoes off and dropping my bag on the ground. "You're my savior."

"No problem-o," Bryson says, twisting his head for a quick peck on the lips. "It's almost ready. I could bake it with some panko, but it's pretty late, I figure you just want to get it down the hatch."

I sink into the chair by our small table. "Yeah, that's fine."

He gets a bowl out of the cupboard, loads it up with cheesy macaroni, and sets it in front of me. I inhale it while he puts the leftovers away, nearly burning my mouth, not even caring how wolfish and messy I must look.

"Wow, Carleigh." Bryson sounds impressed. "That was really something." He finishes cleaning the pot and sets it on the drying rack.

"I was hungry," I say, half-defensive, half-apathetic.

He takes my bowl.

"No judgment!" he says, setting it in the sink. He squirts dish liquid on it and begins to wash it. "So, what was so bad about work today? Just really busy?"

I groan. "Oh, just everything. I like the people I work

with, but I'm not looking forward to going back in a couple months." I take a long sip of water. "First, we ran out of this beer everyone's been raving about, but it wasn't taken off the tap list, so I had to spend the whole night explaining and re-explaining to people that we didn't have it. And yes, it was really busy, so I didn't get a chance to have a break, and by the end, I had this sort of hunger-fueled rage that I had to suppress every time I was annoyed."

Bryson snickers. "I'm familiar with it." He sets the bowl and fork in the drying rack.

I glare at him. "I ended up hitting a customer, Bryson. I'm not in trouble, but he got kicked out, and he said he was going to sue the bar."

"Those people never end up doing that," Bryson assures me. "What'd he do to you?"

I look sheepish. "I sort of overreacted. It was time for me to leave, so I asked if he wanted the check and he reached over and started rubbing the back of my leg. He was really drunk," I add hurriedly, seeing a dark look cross Bryson's face, "I wasn't in any danger, and the bouncers were right on him after, but I couldn't help it - I just slapped him."

Bryson is frowning deeply. His hand is gripping the edge of the countertop firmly; his knuckles are turning white. "Fucking right, Carleigh." He gives me a once-over. "Are you okay?"

"I'm fine. Totally fine. Other than being slightly worried I'll get sued."

"You won't." Bryson's in front of me with one large stride, holding his hand out. "Come on. Let's get you to bed. The ferry to my mom's leaves at ten o'clock. You didn't forget about that, did you?"

"No, of course not. I can't wait to meet her."

I let him pull me to my feet and lead the way to the bedroom. For the most part, we've still been sleeping in our own beds, at least on weekdays; it's part of going slow, as I asked for. It works decently well since he usually wakes up much earlier than me. Weekends have been a different story, with us usually falling asleep in the living room and then trudging to the same bed, but it's been a long day, and tonight I just want him with me.

I strip down to my underwear and an oversized t-shirt that's almost definitely Bryson's, then crawl into bed. He slips in behind me and wraps himself around me. I barely have time to register the kiss he drops on the back of my shoulder before I'm fast asleep.

22

BRYSON

Carleigh will be the first girl my mother has met since college. Carleigh might not voice her concern, but she knows how close I am with my mother, and they need to get along. There are some that say that it doesn't matter if their parents approve, but it ends up causing issues in the long run. My mother is important to me, and she needs to like the person I'm with, especially if Carleigh ends up becoming my wife down the line. She might not beg me to come over, but she still likes me to visit. I pray today goes good.

I'm up way before Carleigh, and take the time to take a shower, and drink a cup of coffee. The closer it gets to nine o'clock, the more I want to wake her, but she did have a late night. It was her final night at Logan's until she returns from Hyde Park, and it only cements her leaving.

Don't get me wrong, I'm extremely happy that she has been chosen for this, but it's three months apart. It could be worse, and be farther than three hours away, so I guess I shouldn't complain too much.

As the clock reads nine, my hand gently caresses her cheek, and she slowly opens her eyes. "I know you're exhausted but we have an hour until the ferry leaves. Time to get up."

Missing the ferry isn't an option, because that would not send a good impression to my mother.

Her body shoots out of the bed and into the bathroom. "Why did you let me sleep so long? How am I supposed to be ready in half an hour, Bryson?"

She can be mad at me, but today is going to be stressful. Carleigh needs all the sleep she could get beforehand. I try to cut down the time before we leave by getting her coffee ready so she can drink it while she gets ready. It's not like she needs to dress up or anything. My mother won't care what clothes she is wearing or if her hair is in a bun. All she cares about is how she treats me and if I'm happy.

Carleigh's family is much different than mine. They are more of a stickler for appearance, and even though they didn't seem to have a problem with me at the marathon, we weren't together yet. Would they even approve of us being together? I don't come from money, and live modestly. All they should care about is that Carleigh is happy, but I'm sure there will be more to it than that. Her father will want to know that I can provide for her, and it might not be a huge salary, but we will manage. I try not to let myself get into my head about this. The day will come when her parents come to town, and we will cross that bridge when we come to it.

The shower starts, and she starts singing some pop song. I take this as my cue to go to the kitchen and start the Keurig.

I put her mug underneath and lean up against the counter when my phone rings.

"Hey, ma."

"Just wanted to make sure you guys are still coming before I put lunch in the oven."

"We will catch the ferry at ten. See you soon."

Am I worried my mother won't like her? Not at all. For years, she has pushed me to find someone, and start a family. Carleigh and I won't be starting a family any time soon, but I think I have found my partner. She always used to tell me she would come along when I least expect it, and she couldn't be closer to the truth. Carleigh and I didn't have a wonderful first impression of each other before we moved in together, but we were both desperate. Sometimes, I wonder what would have happened if I never moved in. Would we have run into each other a different way? Not likely.

Everyday living with Carleigh has given me the ability to get to know her on a more personal level, and she isn't as much as an ivy league girl as I thought. Sure, her parents raised her that way, but she is down to earth. She does worry way too much about what others think, but that comes with the territory when you come from a wealthy family. They expect you to uphold the image, and it's too much.

Her parents didn't come to her graduation, which I'm peeved about, but they were away on a cruise. She is in college for many years to appease them, and they can't even attend her graduation? Carleigh's parents didn't seem like this type to me when I met them at the marathon, but sometimes first impressions aren't what they seem. I spent most of that night trying to celebrate with her and our friends, but they put a damper on her excitement.

The Keurig beeps and I take it to the bedroom, when I hear the shower turn off. She smiles and takes it from me, taking a sip, and sitting on the bedside table.

"So, what should I wear?" she asks, pulling outfits out of the closet. "I really want her to like me."

I think it's adorable how worried she is about this. Carleigh is a wonderful woman, and there is no doubt my mom is going to love her. I point to the jeans and t-shirt. "No need to dress up. Take a breath, babe. She's going to love you."

She smiles, and the towel drops onto the floor, exposing her curves. My eyes travel down her body, and if we weren't already running behind I would make love to her right here. She pulls a pair of white lace panties on, and then the jeans over her figure. Her perky breasts get hidden underneath a black t-shirt. I'm one lucky man.

"See something you like?" she asks.

Carleigh takes a seat on the bed next to me, and places a kiss on my lips. "I'm glad you are taking me today. It shows me you're serious about us."

Did she not think I was serious before? Does she think I'm going to run away? Listen, there are obstacles in every relationship, and sure the distance will suck, but there isn't a damn thing that is going to warrant losing her. We are going to make it, distance or not.

"Baby, I'm not going anywhere. I don't want you to get in your head about Hyde Park. If I wasn't the type to sleep around before you, then I'm not the type to do it while you're away. You trust me, right?"

She nods and takes another sip. "With all my heart, Bryson."

On that note, she gets up from the bed and strides into the kitchen, pouring the remainder of the coffee down the sink and washing the mug.

"Let's get a move on. If we miss this ferry, we are screwed!"

I grab my flannel, and follow her out the door and down the elevator.

One thing about my mother is she has worried about me being alone. She doesn't think it's healthy. She comes from a very old-fashioned time, so I try to be nice about it, but things happen when they are supposed to. Rushing things aren't going to help anyone. I know she is going to ask about marriage and babies today, but I hope she doesn't intimidate Carleigh. We are young and still have our whole lives ahead of us, and rushing into those things can't ruin a relationship. We have to get comfortable walking before we start to run. Cliche as hell, I know, but it's the truth.

We make it with a couple minutes to spare before the ferry leaves, and we find a spot on the backside so we can see the view while riding over. It's a little chilly outside, but nothing my flannel and her cardigan can't handle. I pull her close, and put my arm around her as we drink in the view.

"Have you ever been on the ferry over here?" I ask, and she shakes her head. "Well, this will be a treat for you."

The ride over is beautiful and my eyes are mostly watching her reaction. Seeing the skyscrapers from far away, with the skyline in the background, it's breathtaking. I've seen it a million times because of the commute, but for a first-timer, it's hard not to just drink it in.

The ferry comes to port, and we exit. She looks around, and isn't happy when I tell her it's about a mile walk to my mother's house. Carleigh acts like she didn't just run a damn marathon. She laughs, and takes my hand.

We are going to be just fine. I have no doubt about it. Our personalities are so different, and that's why we are getting along so great. We complement each other in ways we could have never seen. Our pairing is weird from the outside, but just right to us.

She drinks in the neighborhood, the kids running around playing outside, and how clean it is. It's nothing like Hell's Kitchen. The people here like to take care of it. Seldomly do you find litter on the roads.

We make it onto her street, and my chest rises and falls. Why am I nervous? They are going to love each other. Carleigh treats me well, and that's all my mother wants.

When we get to the front door, Carleigh pulls on my hand and stops me before knocking.

"Are you sure she's gonna like me?"

I kiss her, nod and then knock.

The door opens, and my mother envelopes me into a huge hug, pulling me inside, and my hand is still entwined with Carleigh's.

"You must be the woman he has been telling me so much about," she says, bringing her into a hug, too.

Carleigh's shoulders relax and she smiles.

23

CARLEIGH

The need to impress is on, and it's not exactly how I had our last two days together planned, but meeting his mother is a big deal. She insisted we have lunch today before I head out to Hyde Park, and who am I to decline? Bryson is a stand-up guy, and who wouldn't want to meet the woman that raised him? I look over at Bryson before following his mother into the kitchen.

"Have a seat, guys."

We sit down at the table, and my eyes search around the area. There are a bunch of old pictures and Bryson catches me.

"That's my father. He died when I was twelve. Massive heart attack," he says, gripping my hand.

Bryson hasn't mentioned his father, and I just assumed that he ran out of his mom, but a heart attack? The way he is with women, you can tell he spent most of his time with them, and his mother seems to be very sweet. I never asked about his father because it's not good to drudge up the past. He would tell me about him eventually.

He tugs on my hand as he stands up, and walks me into the living room to look at more pictures.

"My mother has a hard time talking about him. It's almost their anniversary and that's when the depression hits every year. She has never had another man in her life."

Now that's love right now. When you can't imagine anyone else in your life.

His mother walks into the living room. "So, I'm making my famous lasagna. It'll be down in about ten minutes or so. Let's chat, shall we?"

So, we sit back at the table, and she stares at me. I'm not sure how to take this. Is she contemplating what to ask me? Does she think I'm not good for her son? A mother can be very protective of her son, and I just want her to know how much I care for him.

Bryson is twiddling his thumbs, and just glances at both of us. Our eyes are deadlocked. Then the questions start.

"So, what finally made you want to date my son? I know he has liked you for a while…"

I look over at Bryson, and wonder how long? His mother seems to think it's been a while, and honestly I didn't even catch on until the marathon. Maybe a little earlier, but I thought it was all in my head.

"Your son is a great man, and honestly, I never trusted my gut. I'm a hard girl to handle, and usually people don't tend to stay around for long."

"And why is that, dear? I haven't heard a single bad thing about you?"

Bryson excuses himself to take a call from the construction site.

"I'm a little OCD and very driven. When I have a goal, I don't give up until it's achieved. My friends tell me I'm intimidating."

His mother taps on the table. "There's nothing wrong with that. In fact, that's something that Bryson needs. Tell me about your family."

This isn't something I planned to talk about today, but she asks. My family does come from money, but I don't let that define me. I want to find my own way in the world without their help. Or my last name paving my way. She nods, and lets me continue. One thing I know, whatever I achieve is because I worked my ass off to get it. I don't need or want handouts. On the contrary, to what my parents might think.

"I think you guys are going to make it, but please don't break my son's heart. He says you are leaving for Hyde Park on Sunday?"

I nod.

"Just make sure you come back to him. He is a loyal person, and sometimes he can get taken advantage of, and I'm hoping that's not the case with you."

He has told me about some past relationships where they hadn't been as forthcoming about things, and it didn't end well. I'm not like the other girls he has been with, and I pride myself on being honest.

Bryson comes back in just as the timer on the oven goes off, and he grips my hand.

"You okay?"

I smile, and give him a kiss while she pulls the lasagna out of the oven.

"Bryson is like no one I have ever met, and honestly, I'm scared he is going to find someone better. However, I am going to try to be the best girlfriend possible for him. Show him how I care every day."

She smiles and nods. "I like her. She's honest and doesn't deter easily. Most girls would have waited to meet me."

Bryson laughs. "You can be kind of intimidating. Her father is gonna tear me to shreds, I'm sure."

My father is someone who believes I should be with someone of the upper class, but he doesn't get to choose. It's my life, and my future. Bryson is the person I want to be with and he will come to accept that.

"Bryson, if someone can't see what a catch you are, don't beg. I'm sure Carleigh here has told her dad about how you treat her, and that's all any parent wants. To know their child has someone."

She makes three plates and sits them on the table.

After we finish eating, she asks me about my plans for the future, and mentions my love for baking. It's funny that after all the time I spent on getting my master's degree, my dream is to own my bakery. My parents aren't going to like it, but it's what I want. As I get older, I have to stand up for myself and my dreams. My father might want me to become a professor, but I shouldn't plan my future on what he expects. I've done everything they have asked up until this point, and now it's time for me to carve my own path in the world. That all starts in Hyde Park.

"You sound like you know what you want. Don't let anyone tell you what you need to do with your life. You sound like a smart girl, and living your dream is going to bring you so much happiness. Do something you love, and you'll never work a day in your life."

The conversation takes a turn when Bryson and her start talking about real estate, and that's something I know nothing about, and I just sit back and relax. He has mentioned her wanting to branch out into Manhattan, and do some more investments, but it's a tough market.

"So, are you guys going to get a bigger place? Possibly in a better area? I worry about the crime out there." Her eyes land on mine. "It's not the best area to have a family."

Bryson throws his hands up. "I knew you were going to bring it up. Mom, we haven't been together that long. Let us get our feet wet before you ask us to jump in head first."

I love his analogy. Do I want to have kids someday? Yes, but it's important for us to be established before doing so. My dream of opening a bakery is going to take time and effort to make it a success and it's hard to do all that with a baby in tow.

"Let's hear from her, son."

I didn't expect to have this conversation in public, but she's not getting any younger, and it's apparent she wants grandchildren.

"I want to have a nice home and have things in place before we have any children. It'll be at least five years. Starting a bakery isn't a sprint, it's a marathon. The hours I'm going to have to put in are going to be exhausting."

Bryson is going to be an amazing father someday, I have no doubt about it, but there is no point to rush. We are young and have our whole lives ahead of us. We need to take this one step at a time right now.

This topic must frustrate Bryson because he gets off the couch, and makes some excuse about having a reservation for dinner back in the city, and we need to catch the next ferry to make it.

"Oh, son. I'll stop."

He swears we have a reservation and when he shuts her door behind us, he sighs.

"I'm so sorry. Kids and marriage isn't something I wanted you to be bombarded about. Don't feel pressured. I'm not ready for kids yet. We are just getting to fully know each other, and I don't want to bring kids into the mix until we are ready."

I smile and give him a kiss before we head to the port.

"So, what is it about this reservation?"

He laughs, and swats at the air. "There isn't one. I just wanted to get you out of there."

Bryson is someone I can see a future with, and it might scare me but I'm not pulling away from the one of the best men I have ever had the pleasure of knowing.

I love Bryson for all his quirks, and wouldn't have it any other way.

24

CARLEIGH

I sleep until almost ten.

The only reason that I even wake up at that point is because my phone starts ringing. I pick it up, bleary-eyed, and presses ignore with an audible groan when it's obvious that it's a spam caller. I glance at the time, give a grand stretch, and slide out of bed.

I use the bathroom and brush my teeth, glad for some clean relief from the taste of late-night macaroni that's still in my mouth, then shuffle down the hallway barefoot to see where Bryson is.

I find him in the kitchen with a pile of farmer's market mini cucumbers and several jars for pickling already prepared. He's in a light blue t-shirt and a pair of shorts with his favorite baseball cap perched backwards on his head. Bruce Springsteen is playing quietly from his phone's tiny speakers, and he's humming along with a smile on his face.

I walk up behind him and slide my arms around him, pressing my face to his back. "Hi," I say, muffled and sleepy.

He covers my hands with his own. "Morning, babe," he greets, unwinding my arms from him so he can turn around to face me. "Sleep well?"

I nod and yawn. "I need coffee."

Bryson tilts my chin up and kisses me. "Want me to make it for you?"

I shake my head. "No, I can do it." I shuffle to the end of the kitchen where the coffee maker and grinder are, and reach up to the cupboard where I keep my beans. I set the bag of coffee down on the counter when Bryson's arms slip beneath my arms and circle around my waist.

"You're so pretty," he mumbles into my hair.

I lean back into his chest, still sleepy and pliable. "I look like a mess," I point out. "I've been past a mirror."

His left hand drifts beneath the hem of the t-shirt I'm wearing. "You must be looking in a different mirror than I am."

"I don't think so," I say, but even while I'm speaking, my chest is arched into his hand. I'm not sure if it's the memory of my bad shift last night or the comfort food he made me or his general, overall sweetness, but I'm feeling needy today. "Bryson, that feels so nice."

Bryson's right hand joins in, tenderly fondling my other breast. He massages them gently, occasionally flicking his thumbs over my nipples, and latches his mouth to the side of my neck. "I want to make you feel good, Carleigh."

He's hard against my lower back, but he's still so gentle; it feels good, but I'm not sure if that's what I need right now. So, I tilt my hips backwards against him, and in response, he presses himself against me and squeezes my breasts harder. "Fuck, Carleigh," he mutters, dropping one hand from beneath my shirt so that he can slide his palm over my ass.

"I didn't do anything," I whine, wiggling my hips.

He pulls the cheek of my panties to the middle, exposing more of my skin, and slaps my ass. I bite my lip against a moan, but gasp audibly when he does it again. He rubs one of my nipples between his thumb and forefinger, then drops his hand and tugs my shirt off from the hem in one swift motion.

I'm awake now, coffee be damned. Bryson tugs my underwear down my panties pool at my ankles, and I kick them to the side. He slides his right hand between my legs, teases two fingers at my entrance, and holds my hips from moving with the other arm. I grip the countertop and try to breathe steadily.

"Still think you're innocent?" he asks over my shoulder, as his fingers begin to slowly enter. "Because I don't think so, Carleigh."

I can't help it; I whine and press my ass into him. Bryson tugs my head to the side, drags his teeth over the side of my neck, and thrusts against me in response. His fingers push deeper, thumb beginning to circle my clit, and oh god, oh god, this time I don't want just this. This time I want all of it, all of him.

"Bryson," I breathe, grabbing his right wrist in my hand to still its movement.

He pauses, fingers still inside, and kisses my ear. "Yeah, baby?"

"I'm ready," I say breathlessly. "I'm ready, I don't want to wait anymore."

Bryson's forehead presses against the side of my head.

"Carleigh," he says, his voice gravelly. He cups my left breast with his hand, rolling it gently in his large palm. "Are you sure?"

I place my left hand on top of his and push him to squeeze me harder, to leave a mark, to cover me and fill me like I want. "I'm sure," I answer softly. "I want you inside me."

His lips find my ear again. "Okay," he says simply. He lets go of my breast and slowly removes his fingers from inside, then turns and scoops me into his arms. I hang onto his neck and giggle nervously, suddenly finding it amusing that he's fully clothed and I'm completely naked.

Bryson walks us into my bedroom and sets me down on the bed. He takes off his shirt, but he doesn't make a move to take his pants off. I watch, curious, as he walks out of my bedroom and presumably into his. He returns a moment later with a condom and sets it on the corner of the bed.

Then, just as he kneels on her mattress, he grins.

I can't help it; I laugh, feeling delightfully not self-conscious, feeling free, feeling happy. "Come here, Bryson," I demand, reaching for him.

We kiss for a while, slowly at first, and then with more fervency as we regain some of the momentum we lost in the transition to the bedroom. His hands, it seems, are everywhere; we've already seen each other naked and I've come around his hand multiple times but somehow it's like he's cataloging me for the first time, anyway. Bryson drags his mouth away from mine and starts mapping my curves with it, lapping at my neck and my breasts and even swirling his tongue into my belly button before it makes me giggle too much and he has to stop. He talks as he goes, of course, telling me the things he loves: "Love your neck, Carleigh," "love these pretty tits," "love your stomach, babe, and you taste so good in here," with the last comment punctuated by his tongue sliding onto me.

"Need you to be ready for me," Bryson is saying, as I watch him hook my knees over his shoulders.

"Hmm," I respond, feeling dazed, and then he's not talking anymore, finally, that big mouth being put to good use. He's done this before and he's pretty good at it, not that I have a tremendous amount of expertise, but he seems to know where I need him, when I need him to slide a finger inside, just how to purse his lips around my clit.

I knock his hat away with my hands, feeling desperate as the coil tightens in my abdomen, and drag his unkempt curls between my fingers. I've always felt so vulnerable with oral sex, so anxious about letting anyone have this much control over me, but things feel so different with Bryson. I feel so comfortable, so relaxed, so taken care of, so worshiped as his hands grip my ass and he plays me with his lips and his tongue.

I come hard with two fingers inside and my clit between his lips. I lay there, boneless and smiling, only somewhat aware of the sound of his shorts falling to the floor. There's the tearing of a foil packet and then Bryson is there, up at my face, kissing me. I can taste the remnants of myself on his tongue and it does something inside me; I clutch his shoulders and kiss him harder, and when he bends my knees and spreads them again, I'm ready.

Bryson pushes into me slowly, his breath staggered, his body trembling with control. "Oh fuck, Carleigh, baby you feel so good -"

I'm inhaling slowly, relaxing my muscles with closed

eyes, focusing on my breath as my smaller body stretches to accommodate him. He's big, bigger than I thought he'd feel like. It's painful, almost, a hard stretch but a good one, and finally I roll my hips up to get him to move.

"Bryson," I breathe, opening my eyes to look at him. He's gazing down at me with concentration etched into his furrowed brow but his eyes full of love and adoration. "Come on, Bryson," I urge, increasing our pace.

He drops to one elbow above me, his hips still moving, one hand keeping my left leg bent at the knee and pushed away to give himself room. I'll have sore thighs later, but it'll be worth it.

Bryson pushes deeper, his eyes dropping from mine when his thighs tense. He reaches between them to touch me, but I'm so sensitive and spent and I just can't, so I drag that hand up to cover my breast instead and then kiss him.

Something about my tongue in his mouth seems to really do it for him, because his hips quicken and my thighs ache and when I clench around him he comes, his groan escaping into my lips. He pulses into me once - twice - afterward, then drops his head beside mine and kisses the shell of my ear.

"You're so amazing, Carleigh," Bryson says quietly, his voice rough but gentle. He feels hot when he pulls out of me, and I immediately sense the loss when he steps away to discard the condom. Then moments later, he's back with a cloth, cleaning me up.

I roll onto my side to give him room to join me. I should get up and pee, should actually clean up a bit, probably need a shower anyway - but then Bryson's in bed behind me and his arms are surrounding me and there's a blanket involved now and this is so, so much and just enough at the same time.

"You making me breakfast later, Half-Sour?" Bryson murmurs into the quiet room, the distant sounds of Bruce Springsteen filtering down the hallway from the kitchen, where it still plays on his phone.

I settle back into him, smiling. I bring one of his hands to my mouth and kiss it. "Nap for twenty-minutes with me and I'll make you anything you want," I promise.

"Not picky," he says. "Got lots of fresh veggies at the market though, and got some farm eggs."

"Harvest omelet," I say, my eyes nearly closed again. "Good time of year for that."

As the time approaches for me to leave for Hyde Park, my stomach tightens, not knowing if what we have is going to survive. Is Bryson okay with only seeing me on weekends?

"So, we should really talk about my moving to Hyde Park. Do we need to put this on pause while I'm gone?"

It's not what I want, but I don't want him to feel trapped. Sure, I'm only going to be three hours away, but distance doesn't always make the heart grow fonder. Am I scared that by the time I'm down with this opportunity, he might have found someone else? Yes, but I try to push that doubt far away and focus on what we have. Neither of us saw this coming when he moved in, and as much as it took us by surprise, right now there is no turning back. Bryson is someone I want in my life, but I can't let him stray me from things that I want to accomplish. No more than I would stand in the way of something he wants to do. If Bryson and I are going to survive long-term, we have to understand this from both spectrums. Believe and trust each other.

He comes over and tucks my hair behind my ear. "There is no pausing what we have. I will be anticipating seeing you every weekend until you are back in this apartment with me. I've never thought much about my future, but I do know that I want you in it. I love you, Carleigh."

ABOUT THE AUTHOR

Ashley Zakrzewski is a USA Today & International Best Selling Author known for her captivating storytelling, sultry plots, and dynamic protagonists. Hailing from Arkansas, her affinity for the written word began early on, and she has been relentlessly chasing after her dreams ever since.

You can stay up to date with her releases and giveaways at www.ashleyzakrzewski.com

You can see all of her books at books2read.com/ashleyzakrzewski